KW-051-374

MAGENTA MAGIC

Heather Graves

WARWICKSHIRE
COUNTY LIBRARY

CONTROL No.

CHIVERS

British Library Cataloguing in Publication Data available

This Large Print edition published by AudioGo Ltd, Bath, 2011.
Published by arrangement with Robert Hale Limited

U.K. Hardcover ISBN 978 1 445 83688 1
U.K. Softcover ISBN 978 1 445 83689 8

Copyright © Heather Graves 2010

The right of Heather Graves to be identified as author of this work has been asserted by her in accordance with the Copyright, Designs and Patents Act 1988

All rights reserved

Printed and bound in Great Britain by
MPG Books Group Limited

MAGENTA MAGIC

0133821465

PROLOGUE

Holding her breath to keep the tears inside, Alexis stared at her wedding dress, hanging on the back of the door. It was the most beautiful gown she had ever possessed; layer upon layer of cream and white silk, trimmed with the vintage hand-made lace which was all that was left of her own great grandmother's wedding dress. It was doubly hurtful to remember how happy she'd been as the dressmaker—or 'worker of miracles' as her cousin Jennifer liked to call her—draped and fashioned it on her body. How could her whole world fall out of focus so quickly, her happiness drifting light years away? How naïve she had been to be so easily fooled.

'Oh, Alex, you're going to look fabulous— like a princess.' Jen had been so supportive and enthusiastic. Like everyone else, she was used to seeing Alex in work clothes—the jeans and T-shirts she always wore around horses. 'I'd no idea you could look so—so—'

'What?' Alex had prompted.

'So regal and glamorous. All you need is a powdered wig an' you'd be the spittin' image of Marie Antoinette.'

'I don't think so. Look how that ended for her.' Alex had giggled. The future beckoned, golden and inviting; nothing could dampen

1

her spirits that day.

Looking back on it now, she wondered if Jen's words had been some kind of omen. Now that her wedding day was upon her, she really did feel as if she were going to her doom.

If only she could turn back the clock; if only she hadn't seen them. But she had and the image was fixed in her memory now, giving a fresh stab of pain whenever she thought of it.

Fingering the silken folds of her dress, she was still reluctant to get into it although she knew it was long past time. It might well be the custom for a bride to be late but her behaviour now was against all reason. This should have been the happiest day of her life but somehow it wasn't. Half-formed thoughts scurried through her mind like rats in a maze and she closed her eyes, trying not to give in to unreasonable panic. If only she had more time. Time to think.

Hearing voices on the stairs, she darted across the room and bolted the door, grateful that she had made her bedroom a little bastion of privacy when she first came home from boarding-school. Right now she didn't need Jen, her only bridesmaid to remind her how fortunate she was to be marrying Jared Allen. A life of privilege awaited her; materially she would want for nothing.

'Alex, I hope you know how lucky you are to have Jared,' Jen had sighed after meeting him.

2

'He's so gorgeous and sexy. I can't help being envious and wishing that I was you.'

At this precise moment Alex wished it were Jennifer, too.

She stared at her unfamiliar reflection in the mirror. Jen had pulled back her curly, midnight-black hair and pinned it under a false chignon. She had then made up her eyes dramatically to make them look larger, the lashes extended with thick mascara and surrounded by kohl. There was a time when she would have been thrilled to see this new, glamorous version of herself but not now.

If only she could have a word with Dad. She knew he would understand. He might even be able to help her to find a way out that wouldn't alienate everyone. But it was rare, these days, for her to have the chance to talk to him alone. Not like in the old days when they used to discuss everything over a large and leisurely breakfast—the good old days before the arrival of Mim. This wasn't the first time Alex wished her stepmother had never come into their lives, forcing a wedge between herself and Vere, her father. A poor substitute indeed for her mother, Marianne, who had died so suddenly, leaving them both alone. Marianne, who was never without a smile on her lips and an encouraging word; unlike Mim who seemed to bring out the worst in everyone, especially Alex who could never fathom what her father had seen in this sharp-

3

faced, mean-spirited woman who was now carrying his child.

As if thinking of Mim had conjured her, there was a rattling of the door handle, followed by an impatient knocking on the door.

The harshness of Mim's voice made her wince, the staccato tones painful as tacks being hammered into her head. 'Alexis! I know it's traditional for the bride to be late but this is beyond a joke. What are you doing in there?'

'Is—is Dad there? I need to talk to him.'

Mim tutted and Alex could imagine her pursing her thin lips. 'Not now, Alex. We're running out of time. Your father is downstairs waiting for you—you can say whatever you have to say to him in the car. Do you want me to come in and help you with your dress?'

Alex couldn't think of anything worse. 'No! No, thank you. I'm almost done,' she lied. 'Just ask Jen to come up and help me with my hair. I messed it up when I put on the dress.'

'Trust you,' Mim tutted again, but Alex was relieved to hear her stumping down the stairs as she called out for Jen.

'Instil some sense of urgency and help her to get a move on, Jennifer. Jared will be thinking she's stood him up.'

Alex closed her eyes. *If only it were possible. If only she dared to do that; to stand him up.* But no. That was unthinkable. After all, her

4

whole life was tied up with Jared's family and her beloved Magenta. She couldn't bear to be parted from that beautiful filly.

She opened the door just sufficiently to let Jennifer squeeze in. She didn't trust Mim not to sneak in behind her.

'What's going on?' Jen peered at her, quick to sense that all wasn't quite as it should be. 'A last minute attack of bridal nerves?'

'Oh, I wish.'

'Come on, Alex, let's get you into that dress and on your way before your stepmother has a spasm. She's red as a turkey cock.'

'I know. Pregnancy doesn't suit her and her blood pressure's haywire. Maybe she'll trump the day by having the baby early and I won't have to get married at all.'

'You *are* in a strange mood, aren't you? What's up?'

'Nothing. And Mim's right. We're out of time.' Alex held her breath as Jen eased her into the dress, pulled up the zip and quickly turned her attention to the voluminous veil, securing it to the bride's head.

'There!' She stood back to admire her handiwork, nodding her satisfaction. 'No one can say you don't look the part even if you're too nervous to feel it.' And she opened the door and ushered Alexis down the stairs, gathering up the veil and holding it so that nobody tripped.

Downstairs, Vere stood up, wanting to take

a moment to admire his daughter. It gave him a shock to see her with her dark hair pulled so severely away from her face, reminding him so much of her mother—his own bride. But Mim intruded on even that moment of tenderness, thrusting Alexis' bouquet into her arms and pushing her towards the door.

'Do come on. That limo has been waiting for nearly an hour,' she grumbled. 'Don't blame me if he charges more than he said.' Vere glanced at his wife and sighed, shaking his head. Nearing the end of her pregnancy, her temper was shorter than ever and it was her husband who caught all the flak. Fortunately, she had to get into another car with Jennifer, at last leaving father and daughter alone and in peace.

Away from Mim's abrasive presence, Vere took the time to study his daughter, able to see at once that all wasn't well.

'Alex, what's wrong? You're so pale and tense—not my idea of a radiant bride. If you're having second thoughts, tell me now. I don't want you pushed into anything against your will. Wedding arrangements are like machines that take off on their own, dragging everyone with them. If you have any doubts now, you shouldn't go through with it.' He gave a wry smile. 'Believe me, there's nothing I don't know about getting married in haste.'

'Oh, Dad.' She took his hand and squeezed it. This was the first time she had heard him

6

come close to criticizing Mim.

'Do whatever you have to do, hon. You know I'll back you up.'

'I'm probably just being silly. Last minute nerves. Everything's going to be fine.' Even to her own ears the words sounded hollow.

'OK.' Vere sounded far from convinced.

But there was no time to say anything more as the limo was turning from the main road to the long straight drive that led to the Allens' Cranbourne property on the outskirts of Melbourne. Alex looked across at the huge marquee where the luncheon and reception were to be held and the car drew up behind an extravagant bower where a marriage celebrant and a bank of chairs filled with wedding guests awaited them. The wind had dropped and the sun had come out, making women grateful for their picture hats and parasols. For spring, the day was unduly warm, heralding the heat of the Summer to come.

A buzz of conversation greeted her arrival along with laughter and smiles of relief. Jen stepped forward and took over at once, fussing over Alex's veil and train. Vere gave his daughter's hand a reassuring squeeze before tucking it into his arm as he led her slowly towards her bridegroom to the well-known strains of *Here Comes The Bride*, played by an old-fashioned three piece band.

Under the bower of white roses and lilies, Jared was waiting for her beside Grady, his brother, who was standing up for him as best man. They didn't look like brothers at all, Jared was blond and fair-skinned like his mother, while Grady had the dark, brooding intensity of his Eastern European father. Of course, they were stepbrothers with nine years between them, but most people found it hard to believe they were related at all.

Unused to being the centre of attention, Alex started to shake, suddenly overtaken by nerves. She glanced at Jared and offered a hesitant smile. He didn't return it, greeting her with a hard stare instead, his blue eyes cold as chips of ice. He seemed to be suffering from suppressed rage, a muscle twitching in his jaw. Grady also turned to glance at her but when she gave him a tremulous smile, he quickly dropped his gaze, looking away.

If only Jared had welcomed her, Alex might well have swallowed her misgivings and gone through with it, anyway. But, in a flash of insight, she realized that was impossible now. As recently as yesterday morning, she had been so happy, so foolishly in love with Jared that she was convinced she must be loved in return. God only knew, that's what she *wanted* to believe. But, seeing him now and coming face to face with this stone-faced anger, she was reminded all too vividly of what she had seen and overheard. Even now, she closed her eyes, thinking how much easier it would be to make the right responses and go through with

8

the ceremony. But when it came to the crunch, Alex was no coward. She wasn't about to become a doormat or live a lie. She would do what had to be done, no matter the cost.

Even as the celebrant turned towards them, calling the congregation to order, she threw back her veil, preparing to speak, although her heart was beating so fiercely, she found it hard to catch her breath.

'I'm s-sorry.' She got his attention at last. 'I can't do this. You have to stop.'

She threw her bouquet at Jennifer who was staring at her, open-mouthed, as she tore off the hampering veil and flung it aside. She kicked off her high-heeled pumps and, before the astonished gaze of family and friends, she hitched up her skirts and ran from the scene as fast as her long legs could carry her. Without really thinking where she was going, instinctively she headed for the stables.

CHAPTER ONE

Twelve Months Earlier

Alex punched the air gleefully and printed off the job advertisement she had found on the Internet. It was so exactly what she wanted—a complete change of lifestyle—although she knew her father wouldn't be pleased. She glanced over the printed words to reassure herself yet again.

Strapper required for high profile racing stables situated on the outskirts of Melbourne near Cranbourne. Experience preferred but training would be given to an applicant with the right attitude. This is no job for a clock-watcher. We expect a high level of commitment from all our staff so please don't apply unless you are (a) devoted to horses and (b) prepared to be involved 24/7. First approaches should be made by e-mail to Toby Hart, Stable Foreman. Morrisallen&sons.com or call during office hours—

She made a note of the number, deciding to call. An e-mail application could be too easily discounted or mislaid.

Alex was within days of her eighteenth

birthday and she was looking forward to this milestone. After leaving boarding-school a few weeks previously with a strong academic record, she knew her father hoped she would take a university course and move back home. They hadn't had time to discuss this yet, but she knew it was not to be. Although she wasn't certain what she wanted to do with her life, she knew she couldn't share a home with Mim, the woman her father had married just over a year before. The prospect of another Christmas like last year made her shudder. Even that silly nickname set Alex's teeth on edge. *Mim.*

She could well understand someone wanting to marry her father. He had a nice house at Wonga Park and with quite a bit of land attached—a relic of her grandfather's wealthier days. It was closer to the Yarra Ranges and the wine-growing areas than the city itself but this was an advantage in his business; he made a fair enough living by breeding and training show and polo ponies. In earlier days he had been part of Australia's Olympic show-jumping team until a back injury forced him to retire. Alex shared his love of horses and they had always figured prominently in her life, although she hadn't inherited her father's talent. She was a competent rider, yes, her father had made sure of that but she had never overcome her fear of jumping over hedges and sticks. It all

11

seemed much too high off the ground. Even so, she had a special affinity with the animals they raised and there were no clouds in her life until she was ten years old when tragedy struck their happy little family for the first time.

Her mother, Marianne, returned home from a visit to town complaining of a severe headache and took to her bed. No one realized how serious it might be. Arriving at the hospital only when it was too late, within twenty-four hours she was dead from a massive brain haemorrhage. Alex's father was too shocked and distraught to be of any help to his daughter and she began to feel as if she'd been orphaned twice. There were no grandparents left alive to help soften the blow. Her father's cousin convinced Vere that a girl as young as Alexis needed a female influence and, before she had time to argue against it, she had been packed off to boarding-school.

Lost and homesick as she was, the routines and disciplines of life at school were a comfort to her. It wasn't all bad. She made friends easily and her life had continued largely without incident for the next seven years. She grew up to be long-legged, athletic and good at sport, adding to her popularity with the other girls, although she was always looking forward to the holidays and the time she would spend with her father and the horses.

Common sense should have told her that

12

this comfortable, almost idyllic lifestyle wouldn't last. Although Vere Hay wasn't a wealthy man, he was trim, good-looking in an old-fashioned, wholesome way and with a good head of distinguished-looking silver hair. Still a good catch. Miriam Sumpter had seen this and caught him while Alex was away.

Vere married her discreetly and didn't mention it to his daughter until she came home for the Christmas holidays, looking forward to spending some time with her father alone. As soon as he met her from the train at Spencer Street Station, she could tell something was up. It was unlike him to be so nervous and distracted.

'All right. What's the matter, Dad?' She returned his bear-hug, standing back to look at him. 'You're like a cat on hot bricks.'

'Does it show?' he said, swinging her bags into the back of his Mercedes and avoiding the directness of her gaze. 'OK, I might as well come clean. I have a surprise for you. I hope you'll be happy for me.'

'Happy for you?' She stopped dead in her tracks. 'What d'you mean, Dad?' She hazarded a guess, being flippant and not yet taking it seriously. 'Don't tell me you went and got married or something?'

'Not "or something". You got it in one.'

Alex felt as if the bottom had dropped out of her world. She had known that one day this might happen—her mother had been gone for

13

more than six years now and she had seen many a woman look at her father with that speculative glint in her eye. And certainly he wasn't so old that he wasn't desirable. Like a lot of men, he'd grown into his looks; slightly heavier yet more distinguished in middle age. But she had expected some warning. A bit of time to get used to the idea. She got into the front seat beside him and stared at the shiny new wedding band on his finger as he put the car in gear and rested his hands on the wheel. It was large and ostentatious, this new woman's badge of ownership. She scowled.

'You don't have to look like that, love.' Vere stole a sideways glance at her. 'It isn't a tragedy. All right, I know I shouldn't have sprung it on you like this but it all happened so quickly. You could say we were both taken by surprise.'

'Love at first sight, then?' She said through lips that were suddenly stiff. 'Is it someone I know?' In her mind she sifted through the list of her father's casual and mostly unsatisfactory girlfriends. No one fitted the bill.

'I don't think so, but you might have heard of her. She's quite a well-known journalist—Miriam Sumpter—although everyone calls her Mim. Did a series of articles for one of the Sunday magazines this year at the time of the Spring Racing Carnival—"Horsemen of Victoria". One of her pieces was about me. I

14

sent it on to you, remember?'

'Yes,' she said slowly. 'It's a nice picture of you—I have it still.' She remembered wondering at the time who had made her father smile at the camera with such warmth. 'And . . . you're in love with her, I suppose?'

'I am very fond of her, yes.'

'Fond? And is that enough for you to upset our lives in this way?'

'Don't be so melodramatic. And anyway, you'll have your own life to lead. It won't be so long before you're leaving me to get married yourself.'

'Not me. I don't even have a boyfriend. I'm not even sure I want one.'

'You'll change your tune. When the right man comes along.' He glanced at her briefly and smiled. 'Don't think of this as disloyalty to your mother; it isn't the same. No one could replace what we had.' For a moment he looked almost sad. 'This is more about comfort and companionship—'

'Yeah. Someone to wash your underpants and provide meals on time.' She was surprised at how angry she felt; how betrayed. 'Well, hello! You needn't have waited so long. You could have hired a housekeeper to do that.'

'Alex!'

She closed her eyes, immediately contrite. 'Oh, Dad, I'm sorry. I shouldn't have said that. But I wasn't expecting this and it's come as a shock.'

15

'Don't worry, my darling. You and Mim are going to get on like a house on fire. You'll just love one another. I know it.'

He couldn't have been more wrong. The two women detested each other on sight and the previous Christmas—the first with Mim in her father's life—was a time of strain and misery for all of them; everyone trying to be normal while walking on eggshells, pretending that nothing was wrong.

Alex found Mim unbearably bossy and small-minded while Mim made no secret of the fact that she thought her stepdaughter spoilt, over-indulged and immature. In January, Alex persuaded a schoolfriend to invite her for what remained of the holidays and promised herself she would never spend another Christmas with Mim again.

She flicked the printed advertisement, wondering whether to mention it to her father now, or just go ahead and apply on her own. If nothing came of it, then she wouldn't have anything to confess. Then she reminded herself that she was an ex-schoolgirl without any references. She needed her father's prestige to vouch for her ability around horses. Although she was no star of the show-jumping circuit, she had an affinity with the animals and the gift of being able to settle the most difficult horse. *My little horse whisperer*— Vere had once called her. Would that be enough to get her this job?

16

Another shock had awaited her when she came home this time. Mim had been busy while she was away, having cleared and redecorated her bedroom without consulting her. OK, it was well past time for Snow White and the Seven Dwarfs to stop scampering across her pale green walls, but the transfers had been one of the last links with her mother who had applied them when she was just five years old. It hurt to find them gone. On top of that, she didn't care for the cool, pale lilac tones that replaced them or the dinky, white café curtains that hung at her windows. The room struck her as cold and empty now, more like one you would offer a visitor rather than a comfortable haven for someone who belonged in this home. With a sinking feeling, she realized the emptiness was because all the soft toys from her childhood had disappeared, along with the treasured photograph of her mother which she had always kept on the table beside her bed. Tears started to her eyes as she searched frantically through drawers and cupboards to find them. Yes, her clothes were all there as well as the photo of her mother in its silver frame, lying on top of them in one of the drawers. She set it firmly in its place on the table beside her bed and went to find Mim to ask about the rest of her things.

Mim was in the kitchen filling the dishwasher. 'About time you showed your face.' She said, without looking up. 'If you're going to move back here to live, we need to establish some ground rules.'

'What did you do with my toys?'

'Excuse me?'

'I see you took it upon yourself to redecorate for me during my absence. What did you do with my things?'

'Well, a word of thanks would have been nice. I shall speak to your father about your rudeness and ingratitude.'

'And you still haven't answered my question. Where are my things?'

Mim turned to look at her then, hands on hips. Not for the first time, Alex wondered what her father could see in this stringy, hatchet-faced woman with her wispy hair, cold grey eyes and thin lips. She didn't even have good skin. 'You will be eighteen soon. There comes a time when you have to put away childish things—isn't that what they say? Those old toys were grimy and gathering dust—a breeding ground for fleas. I saved you the trouble of getting rid of them, that's all.'

'But Miriam, that wasn't your decision to take. They were *my* things.'

'Well, I wanted to do up that room and you weren't here to ask.' Mim shrugged, unable to meet her gaze. 'I had to burn most of them, anyway. They were too shabby and dilapidated to pass on to another child.'

Not trusting herself to speak and refusing to break down and cry in front of this

18

unsympathetic woman, Alex turned and ran out of the kitchen and across the yard to the stables.

'Come back here, Alex!' Mim yelled after her. 'I haven't finished with you.'

Alex ran on, ignoring her.

Fortunately, her father was in his office arranging business with a new client. She didn't want him to see how upset she was, especially as he was likely to say she was making too much of it and take Mim's part.

Seeking comfort from an old friend, she went into the stall of her father's old show pony, Hal Hotspur, who pushed at her, whinnying a greeting.

'At least you're pleased to see me, Hal. I'm sorry. I didn't bring anything for you, not even an apple.' She kissed his forehead and stroked the velvety nose. 'I'll make it up to you next time.' She put her arms around him and buried her face in his neck, breathing in the familiar scents of horse and straw. 'Oh dear, Hal, I don't know what to do, I'm so miserable.' She let the tears come then, wiping out some of her resentment towards Mim. Hal snorted gently, as if trying to tell her he understood.

But it was here while she was with Hal that the idea came to her. She didn't want to take a course of business studies, or learn computer skills to work in an office. What she really wanted was to spend her time working with

19

horses—the animals she loved and understood. And if she could find someone willing to offer bed and board as well as employment, all of her problems would be solved at the same time.

When she felt less angry and composed enough to return to the house, the idea of working as a strapper had taken hold in her mind. It wouldn't be easily won—there weren't that many jobs and competition was stiff among boys and girls but her background had to give her a better than average chance. She couldn't wait to get on to the Internet and start looking. She ran back to the house and crept into her father's study, shutting the door carefully behind her without making a sound. She wanted to get on line right away but if Mim knew she was indoors, she would start bleating about needing some help with the housework.

She was disappointed to find there were very few adverts for strappers. Maybe it was the wrong time of year. There were several for places miles away up country but she didn't really want to bury herself in the bush. Then she found it: the Allens' advertisement for a strapper. And she was almost certain her father knew Morris Allen personally.

When she heard Vere return to the house, laughing and pleased with the happy outcome of his business discussions, Alex thought it safe to come out of his study.

'I wondered where you'd got to,' Mim said. 'I'm on my way out to the supermarket before it gets late. You can come with me if you like.'

'No, thanks.' Alex didn't even have to think about it.

'I thought you'd want to choose some things for yourself.' Mim glared at her. 'I'm not psychic—I can't be expected to know what cereal you like.'

'I bow to your impeccable taste, Mim.' Alex returned her stare with a mischievous smile, knowing how it would irritate the older woman. 'I'm sure whatever you choose will be fine.'

'The supermarkets will be hell at this time of year, too.' Mim grumbled. 'I could do with some help getting the groceries into the car.'

'We'll both come out and help you when you come home.' Vere patted her shoulder, not realizing this would irritate Mim even more. 'I want to talk to Alex about her plans for next year.'

'I don't think she plans for the next five minutes'—Mim's eyes narrowed with disapproval—'let alone next year. But never mind—you'll let her do what she wants—as you always do.' So saying, she snatched up the car keys from the table and headed for the door.

Vere watched her leave, shaking his head. 'Alex, could you try to be just a little less abrasive towards her?'

21

She pulled a wry face. 'Sorry, Dad, we just don't get on. We can't help rubbing each other up the wrong way.'

Vere sighed. 'Come on, then. Let's take advantage of this small interlude of peace. I know you're dying to show me that mysterious piece of paper you're hiding behind your back?'

Alex made coffee for both of them first and they sat down at the kitchen table. Watching her father read the Allens' advertisement with a deepening frown, Alex sensed immediately that he wasn't pleased.

'But Alex' he was shaking his head, looking perplexed—'you left school with nothing but the highest honours. Any university would be proud to give you a place.'

'I don't know, Dad. There's loads of clever kids around these days. Kids who *want* to go to university and know why they need to be there. I don't.'

She had to listen patiently while he went on to say a lot more about lost opportunities and the waste of an education.

'I don't understand,' he said at last. 'You have all these advantages and glowing reports, yet all you want to do is work in somebody's stables shovelling horse shit.'

'You must have shovelled enough horse shit when you were young.'

'So I did. But it was different in those days.'

'Not really. Dad, you're the only person who

22

can help me to do this. You know Morris Allen personally, don't you?'

'Not so well as his eldest son, Grady.'

'Talk to Grady, then.'

'But Alex, I was so looking forward to having you home for a while. Mim even decorated your room. She really is trying to please you.'

Alex knew this wasn't the time to set him straight about Mim's actions, so she ignored that remark. She waited a moment before saying anything else, choosing her words with care.

'Dad, let me make a deal with you. Give me a written reference and tell Grady Allen about me. Let me do everything possible to get this job. If, after all our best efforts, they don't take me on, then I'll do some sort of higher education—business studies maybe—whatever you want.' Not liking to lie to her father, she bit her lips, crossing her fingers behind her back.

'Can I be certain you mean what you say?'

'As certain as I am,' she whispered.

'Then it's a deal,' Vere said.

*   *   *

She borrowed her father's old jeep to drive down to Cranbourne for the interview with Toby Hart, the Allens' stable foreman, thinking it wouldn't do to turn up in the

23

Mercedes. She wanted them to think she needed this job. Fortunately, she had tied her hair back securely, so it wouldn't blow all over the place. On arrival, she saw at once that she had made her first mistake, thanks to Vere. While everyone else was in jeans and casual clothes, she felt overdressed and out of place in her crisp, white blouse and dark blue suit with its pencil skirt. Vere had said that for an interview any time, anywhere, she should dress smartly as if she were going for a job in an office. She didn't feel so guilty now about lying to him and making false promises about going to college if she didn't get the job.

Her first impression of the Allens' operation was good—no piles of muck lying around in the yard encouraging flies—and all the outside areas appeared to be clean and well-swept. It was by no means a small enterprise—she could see horses everywhere; some being walked or looking out of stables, as well as others taking a spell in the paddocks beyond.

Toby Hart came out to meet her, introducing himself and shaking her hand. He was a typical, red-haired horseman, bandy-legged and very much as she had imagined when she spoke to him on the phone.

'I hope you won't mind if this turns out to be a waste of time, Ms Hay,' he said, glancing at his watch while ushering her towards his office, 'but since you're here, you might as well come in. Have a coffee.'

'Call me Alex, please,' she murmured. 'Ms Hay makes me think of my stepmother.'

He glanced at her, quick to pick up on the note of bitterness in her voice.

'You have a stepmother too, eh? I used to have one of those.'

Alex didn't want to be drawn into a moan about stepmothers so she changed the subject instead. 'Mr Hart, I hope you're not going to tell me you've already offered the job to somebody else?'

'No, it's not that,' he said. 'But this is really awkward for me.' Before going on, he settled her in the seat opposite his desk in the office and poured her a coffee. 'Look, to be honest I'm only seeing you because your father spoke to Grady Allen.' He paused for a moment as if considering the next comment he would make. 'Grady said I should go through the motions and let you down lightly.'

'Oh, did he,' Alex muttered, waiting for him to go on.

'Our real problem is that this is a tough job that calls for a man. But because of "equal opportunity" and so on, we had to advertise the position as though it were open to all.'

'Well, so it should be.' Alex felt a flash of irritation. 'I know lots of girls who are first-class strappers.'

'Don't worry, so do I. But this here's a monster horse—a rogue filly, built like a stallion and twice as mean. She's already put

25

one man in hospital and he's threatening to sue. She's always trying to bite and if I hadn't kept my eye on her and jumped out of the way this morning, she'd have broken my arm.'

'I see.' Alex thought for a moment. 'And have you troubled to find out why she behaves this way? Was she ill-treated? Before she came here of course.' she added quickly.

'That's at the bottom of it—more than likely, I'd say.'

'OK. Tell me what you know of her history.'

'Alex, as you see I'm a busy man—and there's really no point. I'm sure there'll be plenty of other stables fallin' over themselves to give you a job.' He glanced at her inappropriate shoes and formal clothes. 'A more suitable one—in the office maybe.'

'Mr Hart, if I wanted a job in an office, I wouldn't be here. I need to work with horses.'

'Then surely your father—?'

'I could take care of my father's horses, yes. But then I'd be living at home. I thought you understood about the stepmother thing.'

'So you're saying you want this job just to get away from home?'

'No.' Alex felt herself blushing as, initially, that had been her purpose. But, now she had seen it, she longed to work in this high-profile racing stables. 'You're turning my words against me. Look, Mr Hart, if we're really going nowhere with this, I'll leave and get out of your way. But not before you've told me

26

about this rogue filly, as you call her. If she's really as bad as you say, why don't the Allens just cut their losses and get rid of her?'

'Why, indeed?' Hart sat back and sighed. 'She's a special project of Grady's. Someone tipped him off that they'd rescued a good horse, one step away from the abattoir. She was in a bad state when they found her and she'd been savagely beaten but you could see the good thoroughbred lines were there. From her brands Grady traced her lineage and found she was originally from New Zealand— the daughter of some obscure mare but a well-credentialled stallion named Winter Warlock. We found a photo on the net and the filly's just like him—has the same unusual dark chestnut, almost burgundy-coloured pelt. She's like a red-headed woman and with a temper to match. Morris had his doubts and said it was throwing good money after bad to take her on but Grady's still convinced that she has potential. She was robust enough, in spite of the way she'd been treated and we thought that with sympathetic handling and good food, she'd get over her fear and bad temper in time. Unfortunately, she hasn't. She put her first handler in hospital and the other lads are too windy to go near so I have to deal with her myself. She needs a firm hand and a groom who won't put up with her nonsense.'

'Hmm.' Alex murmured. 'Or maybe not. Can I see her?'

'Oho, I don't think so. I wouldn't like to have to explain it to Grady or to your father, if Magenta puts you in hospital, too.'

'Just let me look at her, please. I promise I won't go in.' Once again Alex crossed her fingers behind her back.

'Indeed, you won't.' Toby glanced at his watch. 'But I need to top up her haybag and see if she needs any water. You can watch, if you like.'

Alex walked behind him towards the big stall at the end of the block 'We used to keep this one for stallions.' Toby explained. 'But Magenta's more trouble than two of those.'

The horse was silent until they arrived at her gate and looked at her. Then her nostrils flared and she reared, showing the whites of her eyes.

'Come on now, you spawn of Satan—calm down.' Toby growled, preparing to go in.

'That isn't the way.' Alex put a restraining hand on his arm. 'You shouldn't speak to her like that. You're scared of her and it shows. You're communicating your own fear and that's what's upsetting her.'

'Easy for you to say.' Toby shrugged her hand off.

Alex had come to the stables prepared this time with several small apples. She felt in her jacket pocket for them and, before Toby realized what she would do, she quietly opened the gate and slipped into the stall

28

beside Magenta.

'My God!' Toby yelled before he realized he should have known better. 'I told you not to—'

His shout made the filly flinch and she reared again, showing the whites of her eyes.

Alex hushed him, snapping back in an urgent whisper. 'Ssh! Hold the noise and just go away and leave us alone if you can't.'

'I want you out of there before something bad happens. Come out now.'

Alex ignored him, focusing all her attention on the nervous horse, trying to calm her. To begin with, she didn't touch the animal, trying instead to communicate soothing and peaceful thoughts. Gradually, the filly relaxed and, to Toby's amazement, quietly accepted Alex's gift of an apple, allowing the girl to approach and pat her neck.

'That's better, isn't it?' Alex murmured. 'Lovely girl.'

'Well, I'll be. . . .' he murmured. 'I never saw anything like it in my life.'

'It isn't so difficult.' Without being asked, Alex drew water for the filly and spread some feed in the trough. Magenta munched contentedly. She might have been purring if she'd been a cat. 'I'll see you soon,' Alex whispered, stroking the horse's nose. 'I know we're going to be the best of friends.' Then she let herself out of the stall and quietly closed it behind her.

29

'Toby, what the hell's going on here?' A man's voice intruded, undoing all Alex's work and upsetting Magenta again. She whinnied and threw a kick at the side of her stall. Toby and Alex had been so involved in what they were doing, they didn't hear him come in.

Alex turned to see a tall, dark-haired man, perhaps in his early thirties, glowering at her, his face a mask of disapproval. She had time to register that he had the broad-shouldered good looks of a film star and his casual clothes were immaculate. He could have been a walking advertisement for the R.M. Williams country clothing store. But he was obviously on the warpath and in no mood to be reasonable. 'Explain yourself, young lady. Who gave you permission to go in there upsetting my horse?'

'No one, sir.' Alex prepared to stand up to this belligerent man, but Toby came to her defence before she could say anything more.

'Never seen anythin' like it, Grady. Blow me, if it ain't some sort of magic she has. Horse-whisperin' magic.'

'Make sense, Toby.' Grady Allen was impatient with the foreman's explanation. 'There's no such thing as horse-whispering. It's nothing but a lot of baloney.'

'You wouldn't say that if you'd seen her. Magenta was practically eating out of her hand.'

'Please, Mr Allen, don't blame Mr Hart. It
30

isn't his fault. I asked to see the horse and was fully warned of the dangers. He had no idea I meant to go into her stall.'

'Then we're lucky there's no harm done.' Grady was still in no mood to be pacified. 'I'd have a hard time explaining to Vere that my horse knocked his daughter unconscious.'

'This is Grady Allen—Ms Alex Hay.' Belatedly, Toby made the introductions.

'Maybe we could discuss this in Mr Hart's office?' Alex decided it was time to take charge of the situation. She could sense Grady was on the point of telling her to leave and go home.

'I'll give you five minutes.' Grady gave her a speculative look. This was Belvedere Hay's daughter, all right. Not easy to dismiss.

The three of them settled in Toby's office again and, away from the difficult horse and with coffee and biscuits in front of them, they started to relax.

'Mr Allen, I have a theory about Magenta,' Alex said. 'Are you willing to hear me out.'

'Make it sharp, then.' Grady smiled. 'I've got new clients arriving in half an hour.'

For a moment, Alex stared at him blankly. It was such a beautiful smile and lit up that stern, rather hawk-like face driving all other thoughts from her mind. Quickly, she recovered herself. It wouldn't do to be caught staring at him like a slack-jawed dummy.

'It's a perfectly simple theory and without

31

any magic about it,' she said. 'Magenta remembers being beaten and ill-treated, most likely by men. Have you ever tried her with a girl?'

'Hell, no. Our girls know what she's like. None of them will go near her.'

'Well, as Mr Hart will confirm, she's perfectly fine with me. I'm not saying that if something scared her she wouldn't lash out, but in my opinion—and I've been around horses since I was born—she needs a girl to look after her and build up her confidence, a girl to ride track work with her and, ultimately, a girl jockey—provided she can train up and trial well enough to enter a race.'

'Unfortunately, that might never happen.' Grady put in.

'Don't give up on her, Mr Allen. Your instinct to let her have one last chance was the right one. She's a big, strong girl and with the right handling should more than justify your faith in her.'

'But how can I know this wasn't a fluke— just a flash in the pan?'

Alex shrugged. 'There's no mystery here— I'll show you. Let me go and see her again.'

Grady looked doubtful. 'Oh, I don't know about that.'

'Come on. What have you got to lose?'

'Me? Nothing. But she's already put one man in hospital.'

'I'm not surprised.' Alex set off towards

32

Magenta's stall, glancing at Toby over her shoulder as she did so. 'He probably called her "spawn of Satan" or something equally insulting.' She was gratified to see Toby wince.

Magenta snorted a greeting as soon as she saw Alex again, quick to search her pockets for a treat. Alex gave her the second apple and whispered to her.

'I know he's looking at you and you don't like it but behave sweetly for me, please, Madge. You'll ruin everything if you don't.'

The horse snickered and playfully nibbled Alex's hair.

'Well?' Alex patted the horse's neck and smiled at Grady and Toby who were watching her progress, fascinated. 'Seen enough to convince you?'

Silently, they both nodded and followed her back to the office where she picked up her handbag, preparing to leave. Almost certain her trap was sprung, she gave them her most mischievous smile.

'Well,' she said, 'you have my opinion—up to you what you do with it. But you're both busy men and I've taken up far too much of your time already. I'd better go.' And she strode towards the door, looking as if she intended to leave—and, if nobody tried to stop her, she would have to do just that. She was taking a gamble and could only hope it would pay off.

'Where d'you think you're going?' It was

Grady who called after her. 'I thought you wanted a job?'

CHAPTER TWO

Getting hold of the job was only half the battle; Alex knew she would have another one to face when she arrived home. She caught up with Vere in his office, studying the computer.

'Well?' he said, without looking up at her. 'Ready to go to college now?'

'Not at all, Dad. You can congratulate me instead. Grady Allen gave me the job.'

Vere turned towards her then, far from pleased. 'He did what? But I told him specifically that I didn't want—' He broke off then, realizing he'd said too much.

'What, Dad? That you didn't want me to work as a strapper or stable hand because I needed to *realize my potential*,' she wiggled her fingers beside her head, knowing how much that irritated him. 'And go to college like a good little girl? It's too late for that, anyway— all the best places will have been taken by now.'

'Not necessarily. With your exemplary record—'

'Forget about college, Dad!' She was shouting now. 'We had a deal.'

'Did we?' His gaze was cool. 'You never

34

meant to honour it, anyway.'

She had no answer for that because it was true. She took a deep breath and swallowed her temper instead. 'I'm leaving. Now. Today. That horse is in trouble and needs me. I promised I'd be there for her.'

'They seem to have managed well enough without you so far.' Vere's tone was dry. 'And you can't have forgotten it's your birthday tomorrow and Christmas just a few days away. Surely, the Allens can wait until after the holidays—'

Alex huffed impatiently. 'You know how it goes, yourself, Dad. Christmas and birthdays don't matter to horses—they need the same things as on every other day of the year—to be exercised and fed.'

'But it's your eighteenth and I've arranged a party already.' Vere looked quite stricken, making her hesitate. 'It was supposed to be a surprise.'

'Oh, Dad.' Reluctantly she shrugged, and gave in with bad grace. She didn't like to hurt him. 'OK. I guess one more day won't make that much difference.'

'And you could ask them about coming home for Christmas as well? I'm sure Grady—'

'No, Dad!' She found herself shouting again. 'There's just no way I'm spending another Christmas with—' The words were out before she could stop them.

'With me, I suppose.' Summoned by the raised voices, Mim had arrived, eyes glittering with interest. So rare was it to hear these two having an argument, it was something not to be missed. 'Don't worry, my dear. I'm as relieved as you are that we won't have to spend another Christmas together.'

Vere looked at his two women squinting at each other with open dislike, wondering why it was that they couldn't get on. Life would have been so much easier for him if they did. Mim was the first to break eye contact, shrugging and returning to the kitchen. There they could hear her cooing and talking to Max, her Jack Russell. An ill-tempered, nervous little dog, Max cared for no one but Mim and was always ready to snap and bite anyone else. Alex loathed him.

'Tell me about this party, then?' she asked, tentatively, hoping it wasn't going to be at home with Mim in charge of all the arrangements. 'I gather it's not going to be here?'

'No. We're taking over the spare room in the local pub—around eight tomorrow. I didn't think it fair to ask Mim to do the catering— I've invited over fifty people already.'

'Fifty? Dad, I've been at boarding-school for the last seven years. I don't even know that many people around here.'

'No, but I do and most of them have kids leaving-school just like you. Even Grady Allen said he might look in with his younger brother, Jared. He's a couple of years older than you, I believe.'

'Jared? I didn't meet him when I went to the stables.'

'No, well. He's probably off to college like you ought to be.' Vere couldn't resist a final dig.

*   *   *

On the morning of her birthday, Vere and Alex were both up early as usual. They had already been to the stables and Alex was taking care of the coffee while Vere made breakfast for both of them in the big farmhouse kitchen. Like all those who care for animals, they were both morning people and this was their time together. Mim never showed her face before nine.

After they'd eaten in companionable silence, Vere presented Alex with a mountain of cards that had arrived ahead of the day, some from old schoolfriends and some from people she scarcely knew—Vere's friends who were to be at the party tonight.

As well as a A$1,000 to treat herself to some clothes which she needed now she was out of school uniform, Vere gave her an antique, dark red amber necklace that had once belonged to her mother.

'Dad, it's beautiful. Thank you.' Tears

37

sprang to her eyes as she kissed him. In spite of his new alliance with Mim, she knew he still missed her mother almost as much as she did. 'I shall treasure it always.'

'Wear it tonight,' he said, coughing to hide his emotion. 'Your mother didn't have much jewellery but the pieces she did have were good.' He paused, as if remembering an afterthought. 'And there is one more thing,' he said. 'It isn't new so it's not really a present. I've decided to give you the jeep.'

'Thanks, Dad.' She gave him another quick hug. 'I was wondering how I would manage without my own car. But doesn't Mim need it?'

'Says it's an old rattletrap and won't drive it. I've promised to get her a new Honda instead.'

Alex nodded, not trusting herself to say any more. She was grateful for the jeep and she did enjoy driving it but trust Mim to wheedle her way into getting a new car. *Speak of the devil and she will appear unto you!* Alex thought, as Mim arrived in the kitchen at nine, right on cue. She presented her stepdaughter with a card saying 'Happy Birthday, Alexis' along with some exotic pink liliums in a pot. They all knew Alex couldn't take them when she left, but she set them on the window sill and murmured her thanks, anyway.

A fresh pot of coffee was made and poured but the joy had gone out of the morning now

Mim had arrived with her unpleasant little dog underfoot, forever demanding attention and morsels of toast. Apart from Mim's indulgent baby talk to the dog, conversation lapsed.

'Right,' Vere clapped his hands and glanced at his watch. 'If that birthday money is burning a hole in your pocket and you want a lift into town, I'll be leaving in fifteen minutes.'

'You're on!' Alex leaped up and ran for the shower.

Ten minutes later, they were on their way, Alex's hair still wet and dripping on to her shoulders. She made up her mind to visit one of the 'trim only' hairdressers in town and have it cut off. If she were to live in a dormitory and give all her attention to Magenta, she wouldn't have time to fiddle with long hair.

Vere left her at the crossing outside a department store in Lonsdale Street and she assured him that she would find her own way home. She didn't want a time limit placed on her shopping spree.

As soon as Vere had been waved on his way and assurances given that she wouldn't be late, Alex looked for a hairdresser, choosing a small salon in one of the arcades.

The hairdresser was a young Goth with dark, spiky hair, clanking bracelets and long, black fingernails decorated with silver stars. Surprisingly, although she had long, rather painful-looking decorations dangling from her ears, her face remained unadorned. She nodded enthusiastically when Alex told her she needed a whole new, easily managed hairstyle. Like all hairdressers, this girl loved wielding the scissors.

Moments later, Alex was regretting the decision as large clumps of her thick, dark hair flew away from her head. She had an impulse to gather it up and keep it but it was already mingling with the previous customer's hair on the floor. This girl worked alone and sweeping didn't seem to be a priority.

Relieved of its length, Alex's hair sprang back into tight, black curls—not at all the look she wanted. And she had forgotten her unusual height. Instead of the spiky, elfin effect that she had envisaged, the short hair against her strong jaw-line made her resemble a young Greek or Roman soldier.

'We could trim it shorter still or try straightening it if you don't like the curls,' the girl said tentatively, sensing her customer's disappointment.

'Oh, it's OK, it grows like a weed, anyway,' Alex muttered, paying an extortionate amount for her shorn locks. The girl had only done what she had been asked to do and it wasn't her fault that Alex now looked like a boy.

She went back to the department stores to look at some dresses. On a clearance rail, she found several psychedelic maxi dresses and a formal, black mini, all reminiscent of the sixties. She didn't want to spend too much on a party dress for one night—she needed new boots and a good pair of jeans to take to her new job.

Studying herself in the full-length mirrors in the changing room, she decided the hair might not be so bad after all. It accentuated her bones and gave her a sharp, rather haughty look, making her brown eyes wide in a perfect oval face. She had never considered herself a beauty but her trim figure, long legs and consequent height made her striking.

Dissatisfied with her appearance in these mass-produced clothes, she left them and decided to do something radical, visiting the posh opportunity shop where she had sometimes found treasures during her holidays from school. Department store clothes, even reduced, would still cost between A$2-300, while in a second-hand shop she might find a prize for much less.

Surprisingly, the woman in charge of the Op Shop behaved as if she were running a boutique. Alex received more care and attention than she had been shown in the up-market department store where the assistants had largely ignored her. She rejected the woman's first suggestion of a strapless leopard print mini—although she was tempted to buy it just to see Mim's face—and also a red jersey that clung to her body revealing every curve as well as the outline of her knickers.

'D'you think we could find something just a little less slutty?' Alex said at last. 'It's my eighteenth birthday party and a lot of my father's friends will be there. I don't want to give the wrong impression.'

'Oh, right,' the woman said. 'I thought you'd be going clubbing. I do have one more thing—it just came in. Haven't priced it yet—I was thinking of saving it for one of my regulars, but it should be about your size. Halter necked georgette in a burgundy red—it'll be about knee length on you and there's loads of material in the skirt—lovely for dancing and great with your colouring. I've got some high-heeled gold sandals to go with it, too.'

'Oh, I'm not sure. I'm tall enough without wearing high heels.'

'Make an exception—they're gorgeous.'

The dress was a vintage model from the late fifties or early sixties. It came in a box with tissue paper, having been dry-cleaned before being put away. It fitted Alex as if had been made for her and the gold sandals were perfect, too. The shopkeeper even found a small gold leather clutch purse as a final touch.

'Fabulous!' The woman enthused. 'Except for the curly hair, you might be Audrey Hepburn in the flesh.'

'I can't thank you enough,' Alex changed into her everyday clothes and held the dress to her bosom, reluctant to part with it even for wrapping. 'What do I owe you?'

'Well, the shoes will have to be thirty and the purse is ten—that's forty dollars. I know you're probably only a student but I'm afraid I'll have to ask you fifty for that dress.'

'Ninety dollars for all of it then—thank you.' Alex could have kissed her as she handed over a hundred dollars and waited for change. This more than made up for the awful mistake of her haircut and she would still have enough to buy some good quality boots and several pairs of jeans to go to her new job.

*   *   *

At home, when she changed into her new finery, although her father thought she looked wonderful and said so, Mim had nothing complimentary to say about her clothes.

'Good grief,' she sniffed. 'Don't tell me that style's coming back into fashion? I remember my mother wearing a dress like that years ago. And you must be nearly six foot in those heels.'

'Great, isn't it?' Alex said, deliberately drawing herself up to tower over Mim who was wearing the plain, black shift that she always trotted out on formal occasions. Having seen better days, it was getting a greenish, dusty look and Alex was tempted to make a catty remark in return but suppressed

43

it instead.

'We should get going.' Vere glanced at his watch, anxious to head off another sparring match between the two women. 'Won't do to have any guests arriving ahead of us.'

The pub was only ten minutes away; large and old-fashioned, it had been there since Victorian times and was one of the oldest buildings in the town. Although it had been completely modernized inside, the original balconies and external features remained.

The party was to be held in two rooms upstairs—in one was a buffet with finger food and comfortable chairs where people could sit and talk while the other room had a DJ on a stage at one end and a polished floor to allow people to dance.

By 8.30 they were wondering if any of their guests were going to turn up at all when suddenly everyone arrived at the same time, making formal introductions impossible. The older people took up the room with the comfortable chairs and the catchy disco tunes soon enticed the younger generation to dance. In the early part of the evening, Alex found herself very much in demand although some of her dancing partners were a lot shorter than she was and she was beginning to regret the high heels.

The music stopped temporarily. She smiled her relief at her erstwhile dancing partner who was sweating profusely, excused herself and

44

went to get a glass of iced water from the bar. It was then that she glanced across the room and caught sight of him. Surely, he had only just come in—she certainly wouldn't have missed him before. Her breathing quickened as she stared at him. The girls at school would go crazy over this one, she thought, but he's actually here at my party. Tall and fair-haired, lounging in the doorway and casting a practised, assessing look around the room, he might have been a younger brother to Jude Law.

Before she could come to her senses and look away, his gaze locked on her own, giving her a frisson of pleasure because it was clear that he found her interesting, too. She allowed him a small smile, praying that she wouldn't spoil it with a blush deep enough to match her dress. It was true, then. Sometimes it happened just like this—you could fall in love with a stranger across a crowded room. Her heart flipped as he didn't look away but smiled in return and came over to speak to her.

'Well, well,' he said, looking very directly into her eyes. 'Where did you spring from? Haven't seen you in this neck of the woods before?' Although he spoke in clichés that might have annoyed her from anyone else, his voice was pleasantly modulated, low and teasing. It sent shivers of excitement down her spine.

She was about to admit she was just home from boarding-school but she didn't want him to think her so naïve and stupid—or even that young. So she just smiled and said nothing, going easily into his arms when he asked her to dance. He smiled again, showing beautiful teeth and she saw that his eyes were so dark a blue as to seem almost purple. And he really did look a lot like Jude Law.

'You've no idea how wonderful it is to dance with someone without having to look down at the top of her head,' he said.

'I know.' She smiled into his eyes. 'I've been dancing all night with people forced to stare at my bosom.'

'And a very pretty bosom it is, too,' he said neatly, making the blush arrive that she had suppressed before. What on earth had possessed her to say such a thing? She could only suppose it was nerves.

He laughed. 'Sorry,' he said. 'Didn't mean to embarrass you.' He glanced around the room. 'Do you know many people here, because I don't? I've been away at college. Not any more, though, because I've dropped out. My father's fit to be tied but I told him I really don't see myself as an accountant, bailed up in an office, looking at figures all day.'

'Oh, my father wanted to send me to college, too, but I decided to get a job instead.'

'Good for you,' he said, without pursuing

46

the subject. He was clearly uninterested in talking about anyone's work. 'So tell me, how well do you know the birthday girl? My brother knows more than he's saying but he's not very forthcoming about her.'

'And why d'you think that is?' Alex said, hoping to draw him out.

He leaned forward to whisper, almost kissing her ear and making her shiver again. 'Because he knows me too well. I have a very bad reputation with women.'

'Oh,' she said again, her heart giving a lurch of disappointment. She wasn't special to him in any way then. He was like this with everyone.

At that moment Grady Allen appeared, tapping him on the shoulder.

'Come on, Jared,' he said, with a smile that to Alex seemed a little forced. 'I'm cutting in. You can't keep the birthday girl to yourself all night.'

'Birthday girl?' Jared grinned. 'And you didn't let on, did you?' He wagged an accusing finger at her. 'Alex, isn't it? Happy birthday then and I'll see you again—sooner rather than later, I hope.' And with a final smile and a wink that made her heart turn over yet again, he was gone. Following his progress on the other side of the room, she was disappointed to see him teasing a pretty, blonde girl, making her blush. Moments later they took to the floor.

47

'I won't be late tomorrow, Mr Allen.' She returned her attention to Grady. Tall as his brother, although he was dark as Jared was fair, he was surprisingly pleasant to dance with, especially to the slower, more old-fashioned rhythms. She followed him easily as if they had been dancing forever.

'Not Mr Allen—call me Grady, please.' He paused for a moment, looking ill at ease and she knew she wasn't going to like what he had to say. 'Look, Alex, I hate going back on my word—it's something I seldom do—but after thinking it over, I've decided Toby was right. It's too late for Magenta so there's not going to be a job for you, after all.'

'Uh-oh, you've been talking to my father, haven't you?' Alex realized she wasn't fighting just for a job but for her independence; the right to take charge of her life. 'Please, please don't do this, Grady. It's not fair to give up on Magenta when I know I can work with her. You owe it to both of us to let me try—even if it's just for a matter of days. Give me a fortnight at least.'

'Alex, I'm sorry. But Vere made it very clear that it's not what he wants.'

'And do you always do what your father wants?' She experienced a flash of temper. 'If you'd followed all of his wishes so slavishly, how many of his decisions would have been wrong for you? Hmm?' He hesitated, letting her sense that she was on the right track.

'All right,' he muttered. 'You win. If it means that much to you.'

'Really, it does.'

'It could end up costing me Vere's friendship but I'll give you two weeks to show us what you can do. I just hope that monster horse doesn't put you in hospital.'

'She isn't a monster—and she won't.' Impulsively, she kissed his cheek, making him stare into her eyes in surprise. 'I'll justify your faith in me, wait and see.'

The rest of the evening passed in a blur. *Happy Birthday* was sung and the cake duly cut and distributed. Alex danced with both Jared and Grady again—it seemed almost as if they were competing for her attention. Or was she flattering herself? Grady was probably just preventing Jared from monopolizing her time?

All too soon, the party was over and Alex found herself thoroughly hugged and kissed by her departing guests most of whom were mellow with champagne. She herself remained sober; having spent so much time dancing, she'd had very little to eat or drink. And she had no intention of giving a bad impression by arriving for her first day of work with a hangover.

CHAPTER THREE

On arrival at the stables, Alex went to see Toby Hart, expecting to re acquaint herself with Magenta and begin work almost immediately. But that wasn't to be.

'Magenta will keep,' he said. 'I've done all that needs to be done for now. It's more important for you to see where you'll be living and get settled in.'

'No, it's OK,' she said. 'I'd rather get started and working at once. My clothes can stay in the car for now.'

'But that's not how we do things here.' Toby was firm. 'I'll introduce you to Matron—Mrs Brookes—and she'll show you around.'

Alice Brookes was sorting linen in the girls' dormitories when they arrived. Toby made the introductions quickly and left. A thin woman, almost as tall as Alex herself, grey-haired and with the severe mien of an old-fashioned schoolmarm, she peered at the newcomer over half spectacles, looking her up and down.

'You'll do,' she said at last and smiled; a lovely, welcoming smile that lit up her face and changed her expression completely. Alex began to like her at once.

'I've put you in a room with Katrina,' she said. 'She's almost as new as you are and painfully shy—she can do with a friend after being teased mercilessly by those hoydens in the next room. Silly girls. Always playing stupid, practical jokes. I sometimes feel as if I'm running a boarding-school.'

Alex had a moment's qualm, wondering if she'd jumped out of the frying pan into the fire. Having just escaped from the rules and regulations of boarding-school, she didn't relish the thought of a similar regime here.

Mrs Brookes showed her into a spacious room with windows overlooking the stables and pointed out the bed, cupboard and chest of drawers for her use.

'Don't worry, Alex,' she said, as if reading the younger woman's thoughts, 'we don't have too many rules here. Only one—and it's not to be broken—we don't like our boys and girls to visit each other's rooms. Mr Morris Allen is adamant about that one. Break that rule and you risk instant dismissal with no second chances. My rooms are next to the girls' only entrance and I'm a very light sleeper.'

Alex nodded, thinking she would have her hands full, taking charge of Magenta, without getting involved with any of the boys. Then she remembered dancing with Jared and her heart lurched in her chest, making her catch her breath. The last thing he'd said was that he looked forward to seeing her here at the stables. *You're an idiot, Alex,* she told herself, snapping out of the daydream. *Romancing the boss's son is the quickest way to get yourself fired!*

She brought her attention back to Mrs Brookes who was speaking again.

'Girls this side—boys in the other building at the end. In between are the canteen, kitchens and also a communal laundry. We employ cooks to give you three good meals a day, but both boys and girls are rostered for washing up. Your turn comes around about once a week but you can always change a shift with somebody else, if it isn't convenient.'

Alex nodded, beginning to think it was going to be *exactly* like boarding-school.

'Any questions?' Mrs Brookes was clearly anxious to leave and get on with her work. Alex shook her head. 'Well, if you think of anything later, you know where I am. I hope you'll be happy here.'

'I'm sure I will, Mrs Brookes,' Alex said. 'Thanks.'

She had just finished putting away her clothes when the door opened and a diminutive, fair-haired girl stood hesitating in the doorway, looking half afraid to come in. She stared at Alex with round, blue eyes. 'Oh,' she said.

'You'll be Katrina,' Alex wondered how much teasing the girl had to put up with because of her name. She didn't look much like a hurricane at all. 'I'm your new room-mate: Alex. I hope you don't mind having to share?'

'No, not at all. It will be nice to have someone sane to talk to instead of those—' She broke off in confusion.

'Hoydens next door? Well, that's how Mrs Brookes describes them.'

'Does she? I didn't know.'

As if their discussion had conjured them, there was a clattering of footsteps and the sound of female giggles outside on the stairs.

'D'you think she's arrived yet? The polo pony man's daughter?'

'Comes from a posh boarding-school, doesn't she? Bet she's a snob.'

'Or a wet week like that Katrina.'

'She won't be a wet week. Taking on Magenta, remember?'

'The horse-whisperer,' someone else sniggered. 'Or that's what Toby calls her. I think he's smitten—'

Alex came to the door to confront them, deciding she'd heard enough.

'Good morning.' She looked at the four girls in turn whose mouths were now round with astonishment, having been caught on the wrong foot. In her new boots she measured nearly six feet and towered over all of them. 'I'm Alex Hay and you seem to think you know all about me. I'd be grateful if you'd reserve your opinions until we know one another a lot better.'

The girl who was obviously their ringleader didn't respond but clapped her hand over her mouth to stifle a giggle. They almost collided in the doorway of their room in their haste to escape from Alex who overheard a stage whisper as the last one went inside.

'But she's gorgeous, dammit. Bloody gorgeous. Why did nobody mention that?'

Alex returned to her own room, closing the door as Katrina applauded silently. 'That's telling them,' she said. 'Good on you.'

'I hope I wasn't too hard on them,' Alex said, biting her lip. 'It's only natural for them to be curious about someone new.'

'Oh, don't worry,' said Katrina who had the remains of a Scottish accent. 'They've had it all their own way for too long. It's high time someone stood up to those bitches and told them what's what.'

All the same, Alex didn't feel entirely happy. It wasn't wise to make enemies when she was about to take on a job where she was going to need all the support she could get.

*   *   *

Reacquainting herself with Magenta proved to be a lot easier than she expected. Although they had spent but a few minutes in each other's company, Alex was surprised to find that the filly remembered her. In no time at all, she was allowing Alex to groom her and even lift her feet to examine her hoofs.

She was introduced to three other lads who

54

eyed her warily, having little to say. The eldest, Bob Langston, was a boy of about twenty and it was clear that Ray and Mike, his two sidekicks, relied on his opinion and usually followed his lead. If Bob saw no reason to be affable to the newcomer, then neither would they.

He was also one of the head track riders for the stables although he was too tall and heavy to be involved in anything other than training. Alex sensed his resentment towards her immediately but was at a loss to understand it.

She applied herself both to her work and making friends with Katrina, and the days passed quickly, running one into another without event. Her probationary weeks were over almost before she realized it, and she was summoned to the main office up at the house, to meet Morris and Grady Allen.

This was the first time she had encountered the head of the clan who was tall and dark as his eldest son although greying at the temples and carrying a lot more weight. He spoke in sibilant tones, retaining traces of the Eastern European accent he had not quite been able to lose. Vere had mentioned that his real name wasn't anything like Morris or Allen, but that he had Anglicized it, changing it into something Australians would find easier to recognize and pronounce.

'Grady speaks well of you.' Morris said. 'He tells me you are a very capable girl.'

'Thank you, sir.' Alex said. So far so good.

'Hmm. Perhaps a bit too capable for the job you are doing. You will not be bored with the life of a stable hand?'

'No, sir. I was brought up around horses and always loved caring for them. Magenta is a smart filly, an absolute treasure. With the right handling, I'm sure she'll be a credit to your stables.'

Morris raised his eyebrows. 'You can control her wilder extremes, then? Make her safe enough for a jockey to ride?'

'Yes, of course.' Alex felt bound to qualify it. 'So long as the jockey's a girl.'

'A girl?' Morris Allen assumed a haughty expression and looked down his nose at her. 'I do not employ women to ride for me—not on race day.'

Alex smiled, having no inkling she might be skating on thin ice. 'Then, unless you want a disaster at the track, I suggest you make an exception in this case. Magenta's not going to tolerate a boy on her back.'

Morris Allen continued to glare at her, his face becoming an unhealthy red. 'Do you—a slip of a girl scarcely out of school—presume to tell me my business here?'

'Now, Pops,' Grady felt bound to intervene. 'You know what the doctor said about getting over-excited. You have to admit that Alex has done a wonderful job with Magenta so far. I think we should take her advice.'

56

'Oh, do as you wish.' The old man threw up his hands and stood up. 'Who am I, after all? Just the person who pays the bills—an old fool who knows nothing.' So saying, he marched out of the room, slamming the door behind him.

Grady winced. 'Sorry about that,' he said to Alex who was biting her lips, unsure whether to giggle or be alarmed by the old man's show of temper. 'My father will only listen when people are saying what he wants to hear. He asserts himself because we know a lot more about this business than he does and it frustrates him. He'll come around in time. He usually does.'

'I didn't mean to cause any trouble—I was only—'

'Telling the truth. I know. But he won't believe in a girl jockey until she brings him a major prize.'

'Why not? Girls have been winning major races in the Spring Carnival over the past two years. He must have seen that?'

'He sees but he doesn't want to believe. Every time a girl wins, he calls it a fluke.'

Alex slumped in her seat, almost ready to cry. 'Without a girl rider, we're finished with Madge's campaign even before we start.'

Grady refused to sink into Alex's gloom. 'Of course she'll have a girl rider. Don't worry about my father—he'll come around.' He smiled encouragingly. 'So how is the filly

57

shaping up, really? You can give me your honest opinion. I'm not trying to catch you out.'

Alex considered this for a moment. 'Well, it's still early days. I've only been with her a couple of weeks. She's fine around other horses, but still reacts badly if she comes across the boys skylarking around and making a noise.'

'Those idiots should know better! I'll have a word with them about that.'

'Please don't. They'll know I've been telling tales. I'm sure it's only high spirits, really.'

'All right. But you're to tell me at once if they get too boisterous, or the teasing gets any worse.'

Alex nodded but resolved to deal with the boys herself.

*   *   *

On her way back to the stables, she saw Toby Hart driving away and remembered that this was Thursday—his afternoon off. This was the quiet time of day in the stables and she was off duty officially, but she decided to check on Magenta in any case and maybe take her for a walk.

Hearing boyish laughter followed by the frightened whinny of a horse, she paused to listen before entering the stables making as little sound as she could. She sensed

58

immediately that, in Toby's absence, the boys were up to mischief and something was going on. Her heart sank as she realized the sounds were coming from the far end of the stables—Magenta's stall.

The three boys were hanging over the gate, one of them prodding and teasing her with a long stick, bursting into nervous laughter and jumping back when she screamed at them, charging the gate.

Alex strode forward, having seen enough.

'What the hell do you think you're doing?'

They turned in unison, wide-eyed, intimidated by her fury.

'Nothin', Alex.' The ferrety-faced Bob was the first to recover himself and answer her. 'Jus' having a bit o' fun.'

'Fun?' Alex was shaking with fury now. She wanted to grab that stick and beat all three of them with it to see how they liked it. 'You think it fun to torment a horse that you know to be highly strung? Have you no sense at all? You could have had her eye out with that stick? Or she could have broken a leg kicking the door.'

Bob pulled a face, looking pained. 'Come on, don't take it so serious. There's no harm done is there?'

'No harm?' Alex stared at him in exasperation. 'What were you thinking, Bob? I was on the way to restoring her confidence. You've probably undone all my good work in five minutes.'

'Sorry, Alex!' the other two murmured, having the grace to look shamefaced. Only Bob remained defiant, refusing to apologize.

'We need to talk about this,' she said, resisting the temptation to scream at them and box their ears. Violence wouldn't help if she wanted to get to the bottom of their behaviour. 'But not here. I'll see you in the canteen for coffee in half an hour. I'll need to settle Madge first.' The filly was stamping and rolling her eyes, too upset to be exercised now.

With the boys gone, the horse began to calm down although she still quivered under Alex's touch and kept snorting through her nose. It took a lot of reassuring words before she was herself again and it was more than half an hour before Alex felt happy to leave her alone.

The three boys were still waiting for her in the canteen, the remains of their lunch in front of them. It wouldn't have surprised her to find them gone. She collected a coffee and joined them.

'All right,' she said, 'is somebody going to explain to me what all this is about? Magenta is my responsibility and you have no reason to trouble her, or even to go near her at all. Why were you tormenting my horse?'

They all glanced at Alex and looked away again, unable to meet the directness of her

60

gaze. She tried another tack.

'You do know that Grady said I was to report it at once, if I found myself in a situation like this?'

'Ooh no, Alex,' the youngest boy, Mike, started to whine. 'It'll be our jobs, if you do.'

'You should have thought of that before. I didn't expect this kind of loutish behaviour— not here. I thought you were all devoted to horses—'

'And so we are. Really we are.' Mike's ears had turned bright red and he looked ready to burst into tears.

'Then how can you justify what you were doing? Putting the life of that lovely animal at risk?'

'If you're looking for someone to blame— why not blame Toby Hart.' Bob broke his silence to speak in low and bitter tones. 'On and on at us about how wonderful—how clever—you were. How you had more talent in your little finger than the rest of us put together. We were jus' trying to take you down a peg. We thought if we stirred the horse up a bit, you might find her as hard to handle as we do—'

'And then what? Your cruelty would be justified if Magenta put me in hospital like that other boy? Grady wouldn't be able to keep her then.'

'It was a spur of the moment thing.' Bob shrugged. 'We didn't think it through.'

'Can you give me any reason why I shouldn't go to Grady Allen at once with this tale?'

Bob sat back in his chair and smirked, stretching out his legs. 'That's what it is, Alex. Just a tale. Toby wasn't there an' nobody else saw what happened. When push comes to shove, it's only your word against ours.'

Alex looked at the other two boys who were now staring at the floor. 'And you two? Are you both comfortable with that?'

They glanced at Bob and shifted in their seats, still staring at the floor.

'I've wasted enough time,' Bob said at last and stood up. 'Got better things to do than sit here listening to some jumped-up girl. Comin', you two?'

But when Ray and Mike remained in their seats, he turned on his heel and left. With a sinking heart, Alex watched him go. She had made an enemy of Bob Langston and didn't know what to do about it.

On the other hand, she was becoming firm friends with Katrina. Once she had overcome her shyness, the little Scottish girl proved to have an impish sense of humour and a talent for mimicry. When Alex told her about Bob Langston and her worries about his animosity, she mimicked him so exactly that Alex laughed until tears came to her eyes and it went a long way towards banishing her negative feelings towards him.

And the following day there was good news.

Grady told her he might have found the right person to ride Magenta. She was a girl who had just completed her jockey's apprenticeship and was now looking for regular work out of Cranbourne. Grady had told her of their problems with the filly but she was still eager to meet with Magenta and find out if they could get on. If so, she was willing to make a commitment and become her regular track rider and jockey. She went by the unlikely name of Tasha Trussardi, making Alex smile.

The girl, whose age was hard to determine, turned out to be as unusual and colourful as her name. Although she wore Levis and riding boots, from the waist up she was all gypsy, wearing a patchwork waistcoat over an old-fashioned embroidered Hungarian peasant blouse and with a multicoloured scarf tied over pink-streaked short blonde hair. Bright-red lipstick on a wide mouth completed the picture.

She arrived mid-morning and Alex liked her immediately, feeling instinctively that she would be good for Madge. Ignoring the curious stares of the other hands who were inclined to smirk at this colourful new arrival, they brought Magenta out into the small paddock at the rear of the stables to see if she would let Tasha ride her around.

Although Alex would have preferred to do this without an audience, Grady Allen turned up with his brother, Jared, and it wasn't long before half the stable hands joined them, including Toby Hart. This was the first time Alex had seen Jared since the night of her birthday party and, although her heart was thumping so loudly she thought everyone must hear it, she did her best to ignore him although she couldn't resist a quick glance. Almost as if he could read her thoughts, Jared leaned on the fence and stared back at her, giving a slow smile as he chewed a straw. Alex willed him to stop. It just wasn't fair.

'Don't you worry Alex, I'm in control here, it'll be all right.' Tasha picked up on her discomfiture and misinterpreted it. 'Although we could have done without so many spectators. I suppose they're hoping to see the horse play up.'

Alex nodded and gave a weak smile as she started to lead Magenta around, asking Tasha to walk on the other side of her so that the horse might get used to her before she tried to ride. All went well until Tasha took full control and sprang up on her back. Indignant, Madge snorted and reared immediately, trying to dislodge her rider and finding it wasn't so easy as she thought. Tasha had anticipated such a move.

Grady muttered something to Toby who ordered the crowd of spectators away. 'All right, lads, there's nothing to see here. We need to give them some space and get back to our own work.' Reluctantly, Bob and the other boys and girls moved slowly away, feeling cheated. Alex knew some of them had been hoping to see Tasha thrown and herself humiliated by Magenta's failure. She wasn't sure if she was disappointed or relieved to see Jared leave with them.

With no audience other than Grady, Magenta calmed immediately, allowing Tasha to urge her into a gentle trot. Gradually, she increased her speed and Alex leaned back against the fence, watching Tasha take her round.

'Wow,' Tasha said at last, when she decided she'd seen enough for one day and dismounted, patting Magenta's neck. 'She's a beauty all right, strong and probably fast. I can't really say until I get her out on a proper track.' She pulled a wry face. 'But she'll need to get over her problem with people. She'll be facing a much larger, noisier crowd when she gets to the course.'

'Yes, I know she's difficult, Tasha.' Alex felt bound to plead on the filly's behalf. 'But you will be able to help us, won't you? You'll befriend her?'

'Ho, just try an' stop me.' Tasha gave Alex a friendly punch on the shoulder. 'I've got no other permanent job on offer so what else will I do? And I've never been one to shrink from a challenge.'

65

When they returned to the stables after Magenta's workout, Alex checked her mobile and saw that her father had left several messages for her to call him. It wasn't like him to be so persistent unless there was something wrong, so she settled Magenta back in her stall and went to sit outside on a low wall where she knew she wouldn't be overheard.

'Alex, I'm so glad you called,' he greeted her warmly. 'Mim and I have just come back from town, from the doctor's office. I wanted you to be first to know—'

'Oh, Dad, you're not sick or anything, are you? Or Mim?' She added late enough for him to know it was an afterthought.

'No, no, this is good news. Or it is for us. I'm hoping you'll think so, too.'

Alex bit her lip, remembering the last time he said he hoped she'd be happy for him; that was when he got married to Mim. 'Just tell me, Dad.'

'It's totally unexpected. A lovely surprise for both of us. Mim's having a baby.'

'A baby? But she can't be. She's too old, isn't she?' The words were out before Alex could stop them and she felt a surge of panic. Pregnancy followed by a new baby would chain Mim even more firmly to her father.

'I know it might seem so to you.' Vere's response was dry. 'But thirty-nine is no age,

66

these days. Lots of women have babies well into their forties.'

'Oh, Dad.' She tried to imagine Mim looking after a baby and failed. The woman seemed far too cold, too abrasive for that.

'Well, if you can't think of anything better to say, I'm off.' Vere himself seemed unusually touchy. 'I'll fill in the gaps and convey your congratulations to Mim, shall I?'

'Dad, don't be like this, please. It's just that it's come as a shock.'

'I don't see why. You make it sound as if we're in our dotage.'

'No. No, of course not. But—'

'Talk to you later, Alex.'

'Wait!' But when she looked at her phone to see if he was still there, she could see that it had gone dead. She would have liked to give way to the luxury of tears but she would have to save them for later. Tasha and Grady were waiting to talk to her about their plans for Magenta.

CHAPTER FOUR

Magenta was about to run her first race. Hoping to keep her debut as low key as possible, Grady had entered her in a mid-week race for fillies at Mornington where it would be relatively quiet and she was unlikely to be spooked by the noise of a large crowd. Alex had an anxious moment when the farrier changed her working plates for the lighter racing plates, but she held on to Magenta firmly and the filly thought better of trying to lash out or cause any trouble. Then later, after grooming her, wrapping her legs and leading her aboard the float without incident, Alex seated herself in the front compartment so that she could hold Madge's head and soothe her. Feeling stressed herself over this first sortie into the real racing world, Alex was grateful that they didn't have far to go and fortunately Madge seemed untroubled by the other horses stationed nearby. Her issues were with humans rather than others of her own kind. Her race was the first on the card, so she wouldn't have time to work herself into a temper on finding herself in unfamiliar surroundings.

On arrival, once she had cleaned her horse after the journey and settled her into her stall, Alex was surprised to see that the whole Allen clan had turned out in force to witness Magenta's debut. Morris was there, together with Simone, his wife, overdressed for the occasion in an ensemble of scarlet and dark green shot with gold—a costume more suited to a gala occasion in town rather than a small country race day. In contrast to the other mid-week racegoers in their drab, everyday clothes, she put Alex in mind of a colourful bird. Grady was there, of course, anxious to see if Magenta would prove his faith in her and even Jared had come along, already involved in animated conversation with Tasha who was wearing the Allens' colours of regal purple and red with stars all down the sleeves.

Alex had not met Mrs Allen before and Grady was quick to introduce her. He needn't have bothered. Simone cared little for meeting the hired help, greeting Alex with a nod and a half-hearted smile. Then she drifted off calling after her husband. 'Morris! Morris! Get me a gin and tonic. I'm dying of thirst here.'

'Sorry about that,' Grady whispered to Alex, as they watched her try to catch up with her husband on heels that were much too high. 'Simone doesn't really like race day, but Morris insists on bringing her with him. She'll mellow when she has a few sherbets inside her.'

'I see,' said Alex, starting to wonder if Mrs Allen had a drinking problem although she knew better than to mention the thought to Grady.

'So.' Grady changed the subject, reaching out to pat Magenta until he remembered she might not like it and drew his hand back. 'How's our girl today? Ready to eat up the turf and show the competition a clean pair of heels?'

Alex smiled, happy to be on more familiar

69

territory. 'We all hope so. She's travelled well and Tasha's pleased with her work so far. What we don't know, of course, is how good the other fillies are going to be.'

'Well, it's only a field of six, so she shouldn't get knocked around too much, or get into trouble.'

'Not her.' Alex grinned. 'She's more likely to be the one giving it.'

It was now time to saddle up. Having done so, Alex led Magenta out into the small mounting yard alongside the course. She had a moment's worry as the yard was very close to the crowd which had grown much larger although it was still quite early. But Magenta walked calmly beside Alex, her ears remaining pricked rather than flattened, indicating curiosity rather than an impulse to lash out.

'Don't look so anxious, Alex.' Tasha smiled as Alex gave her a leg up into the saddle. During the weeks that they had been working together with Madge, they had become fast friends. 'It's time. You have to let the baby go. We've both done all we can to get her ready for this. It's up to her now. All she needs is a will to win.'

'I know that, Tash. But I still can't help feeling—'

'Stop it. Go and watch the race from the stands and try to relax.'

On her way up to join the Allens in the stands, Alex went back over all their hard

70

work with Magenta over the past weeks and hoped it would be enough. Since the Allens had turned out in force, a lot might rest on her performance today. The filly had galloped, cantered and made good use of the swimming pool. There was even a set of false barrier gates at the stable so that the horses could be trained to enter them without getting nervous when they were confronted with the real ones on course.

Down in the mounting yard, one of the clerks rode up on his big grey, offering to escort Magenta to the barriers but Tasha signalled that she would prefer to manage alone. The barrier attendants didn't have to touch her either as she cantered up to the starting gates and took her allotted place like a veteran rather than a filly about to run her first race.

Alex joined the Allens, taking the only seat left next to Jared on the end of the row. He gave her that lazy smile, making her heart turn over, and leaned close to speak to her so that nobody else would hear.

'Why don't you like me, Alex?' He said. 'When you came to work for my father, I thought we were going to be friends. As it is, I've hardly seen you. Disappointing to say the least.'

'Well, you must know how busy I've been—' she started to bluster.

'Don't give me that. Most strappers have

two—sometimes three horses to look after. You have only Madge.'

'Who is a special case as everyone knows.'

'Oh, very special.' Jared took her hand and linked his fingers with her own. 'You're like a mother hen with her. But I think it's time you had some fun yourself. Come and party with me tonight. Let someone else take Madge home.'

'You know I can't do that!' Alex stared at him, appalled. 'She'd kick the side of the float out on the way home.'

Jared tutted. 'Excuses, excuses.' He still hadn't let go of her hand and, aware that Simone had noticed, her brow creased by a slight frown, Alex tried to pull it away. Jared held on. 'All right,' he said. 'We'll make a compromise. I'll let you take Magenta home But after that, you're changing into a party dress and we're going out on the town.'

'Jared, stop teasing me,' she said in an earnest whisper. 'You know you don't mean it. And your mother's looking at us.'

'Let her look,' he shrugged. 'I can handle my mother. Her bark's always worse than her bite. Win or lose, we're going out tonight and I won't take no for an answer.'

There was no time for Alex to agree or disagree as the fillies were off. While Morris seemed only casually interested and his wife was clearly bored, Grady sat ramrod straight and tense, watching everything through his binoculars, muttering encouragement to the jockey even thought she couldn't hear him.

'Oh, good girl, yes! Let her run wide and stay out of trouble. She's got enough gas in the tank to beat all of them.'

So far the race caller had made no comment on Magenta's performance. In fact, she hadn't come to his attention at all. The field rounded the last turn almost as one and entered the straight.

'And the race is still anybody's.' The commentator's voice rose an octave higher as he tried to inject some excitement into the action. 'And yes! Here comes the favourite, Molly's Fortune, who seems to be having it all her own way. But there's a big red horse—the widest runner, Magenta Magic—and she's coming through fast, diving at Molly's Fortune right on the line. Well, folks, it's a photo finish, but from here I'd say Molly's Fortune held on.' And he paused, waiting for the result, along with most of the crowd, desperate for the favourite to win. 'No! It's Magenta Magic who wins by a nose. A twenty to one outsider and ridden by Tasha Trussardi for Grady Allen.'

Waiting to hear no more, Alex raced down to collect her horse and congratulate Tasha, closely followed by Grady. Tasha was pink with excitement as she received their congratulations. 'Just keep on doing what you're doing with this one and you've got a champion in the making,' she said. 'Look at her—not tired at all. With that aggressive nature and will to win, she'll go far.'

'Now perhaps my father will start believing in her abilities,' Grady said, when Tasha had taken her saddle and gone to scale. 'I think he came here today half hoping to see her fail.'

'But why? Why should he want her to fail?' Alex stared at him.

'Because he's old, perverse and likes to be right all the time. He said she'd never be any good and now he must eat his words.' Grady smiled at her. 'Say Alex, why don't you come and have dinner with me tonight? We can make plans for Madge's future.'

'Oh Grady, I'd love to,' she said, suddenly realizing that she meant it. 'But I've half promised to go to a party with Jared.'

'With Jared,' he repeated, his face expressionless. 'Half promised?'

'Grady, I'm so sorry,' she winced. 'But Jared did ask me first.'

'Sure. Yes, of course.' For a second or two he looked troubled and she paused, waiting for him to say more.

'My brother's a law unto himself, Alex. You don't know him as I do. He has all the charm in the world but—' He broke off, shaking his head.

'What is it, Grady?' she prompted him. 'What are you trying to say? Anyone would think you were warning me off. I'm a big girl,

74

you know. I can look out for myself.'

'Of course.' He smiled and appeared to relax. 'You have a good time now.'

On the way back, in the float, Alex had plenty of time to mull over Grady's words. Why did he feel the need to warn her about his brother? Surely not because he had any interest in her himself? She smiled at herself for harbouring such a thought. No. Grady Allen was world-weary, older and way out of her league. In any case, she told herself, she would have more fun partying with Jared; someone much closer to her own age.

Back at the stables, she turned Madge into her stall, brushed her down and made sure she was comfortable and had plenty of hay in her bag. Then she ran up to the room that she shared with Katrina, hoping to find her room mate at home.

'Congratulations!' Katrina gave her a hug. News had travelled fast and everyone seemed to know of Magenta's success.

Alex had a shower and then started rummaging through her wardrobe, although she knew even before she looked that she didn't have anything stunning enough to wear to a party with Jared.

'Got a hot date?' Katrina said.

'You could say that.' Alex smiled and bit her lip. 'Problem is that I don't have anything to wear.'

'Who is it? Who?'

75

'Stop it. You sound like an owl,' Alex giggled, making Katrina smile. 'And I can't go if I don't find something suitable. I left all my good gear back home at my dad's place.'

'Hm.' Katrina said. 'I've got a little black number I dress up with chains. It's not at all new but you can borrow it, if you like. We're pretty much the same size.'

'Oh, yeah. Except my legs are much longer than yours. It'll be like a mini dress on me.'

'That doesn't matter. You have good legs. And a mini dress is just great for a party. I'll even give you a spray of my Fendi Palazzo.'

Just then Alex's mobile rang. It was Jared.

'All set for tonight, I hope?' The sound of his voice set her heart pounding just the way it had done when she had seen him first, at her own party some months before. 'But why did you have to tell Grady? He was bending my ear for ten minutes on how to behave like a gentleman and not go upsetting his staff.'

Alex giggled. She wasn't about to tell him Grady had asked her to dinner as well. 'Is there going to be food at this party?' She asked. 'Because if not, I'll have to have something before we get there. I haven't had much to eat today and I'm starved.'

'Oh, you Amazons,' he said. 'I suppose those gorgeous long legs of yours are quite hollow?'

'Of course.'

'It'll be fine. There's always loads of food at Jon's parties and most people don't bother to

76

eat it.'

'So where is this party?'

'Big house in Malvern. Doesn't matter how many times the parents veto it, Jon always has a bash whenever they go away. It's a fair drive from here, so we'd better get going. Be outside in five. I've borrowed the Merc.' And, without waiting for her to agree, he rang off.

She turned to her friend. 'Thanks Katrina, I will have to borrow your dress. Jared's ready to go.'

'Oh. So it's Jared you're seeing,' Katrina said, a small frown creasing her brow.

'Not you, too.' Alex felt slightly exasperated. 'What is it with Jared? Everyone talks about him as if there's some terrible secret that I don't know.'

'It's not really a secret.' Katrina shrugged. 'Just don't build your hopes up, that's all. He's been out with every girl in the stables. He'll show you a fabulous time and then dump you. Never been known to ask for a second date.'

'And does this list include you?'

'No, it doesn't,' Katrina protested, although a blush was creeping up from her throat. 'I'm just telling you what the others all say. So have a good time tonight but don't expect it to come to anything.'

'I wasn't.' Alex tried to sound nonchalant to conceal her sinking heart. 'Anyway, it's not really a date. We're celebrating Magenta's win, that's all.'

77

Katrina was right about the black cocktail dress. Apart from being a mid-thigh mini on Alex, it fitted her perfectly elsewhere. She borrowed Kat's silver chains and teamed it with a pair of medium heeled silver sandals, applied a small amount of eye make-up and lip-gloss and was ready to go. Before leaving, she paused at the door.

'Kat, I know it's Saturday night and you might have plans of your own, but would you check on Magenta in an hour or so? After what happened with Bob, I don't trust him— and if he sees me go out—'

'Just have a good time and don't worry about a thing. I'll look in on Madge and send you an SMS on your mobile so you'll know she's OK.'

'Thanks.' Alex felt that she could relax at last.

*   *   *

Jared was waiting outside for her, smoking and leaning against his father's silver Mercedes. He threw down the cigarette and stamped on it when he caught sight of her.

'Well worth waiting for. You look great,' he said, giving her a quick peck on the cheek and making her heart thump before opening the door and settling her into the passenger seat. All this attention made her feel like a princess.

78

Aware that his father might be watching them leave, he drove sedately until they reached the highway, asking her to choose some music from the jumbled selection in the car.

'Mostly my father's taste.' He wrinkled his nose. 'Classical music and opera. But hey! He does have *Les Mis*?'

Alex told him she loved *Les Miserables* and soon they were in the fast lane, overtaking everyone to the rousing songs of the well-loved French musical. Jared seemed to know all the words and some of the time sang along, encouraging her to join him. Alex tried not to let her eyes stray to the speedometer, well aware that they were exceeding the speed limit as everyone else was left behind. She kept expecting to hear a siren and blue and red flashing lights behind them but this time nothing happened.

Soon, they were drawing up outside an imposing Victorian mansion in Malvern. Although it was still quite early, there were cars parked everywhere and no room left inside the gates, so they had to find a place some distance away in a side street. Jared opened the car door for her and handed her out, making Alex tease him about all this olde worlde courtesy.

'You can thank my mother for that.' He pulled a wry face. 'She insists on being treated like the Queen. Won't get out of the car at all unless someone opens the door for her.'

'So chivalry's not quite dead?'

'Far as my mother's concerned—no.'

At the mansion, they were about to announce themselves by ringing the bell until Jared saw that the door was slightly ajar. He pushed it open and called out. 'Jon? Hello? Anyone there?'

'Are you sure this is the right place?' Alex whispered. 'It seems awfully quiet for a party. No music or dancing.' As she said this, she realized there was some background music, but it was playing very softly, the singer groaning breathlessly as if she were in the throes of having sex. Muffled giggles came from a distant room. There were no overhead lights on at all, only table lamps in the hall and the flicker of candles from other rooms. Alex couldn't help noticing the pervasive odour of weed. It was quite distinctive and she knew it well. In her last term at boarding-school, two girls had been expelled for smoking marijuana in the dorm.

Eventually, a tousled young man arrived in response to Jared's call. His crumpled shirt was outside his trousers and his eyes seemed puffy and half closed. He blinked at Jared, smiling sleepily as if he had just got out of bed.

'Wow, man. You made it.' He slapped his friend on the shoulder and took a step backwards to look Alex up and down,

80

appreciating her long legs in the mini. 'And you brought us another fantastic girl. A different one every time. How do you do it? Where do you find them all?'

'Uhuh. Hands off this one, Jon.' Jared shook his head, placing a protective arm around Alex's shoulder. 'She works for my father.'

'So what?' Jon gave a lopsided grin. 'That's never stopped you before. Come on in.' He started ushering them towards a lounge. 'Meet some of the others and then you must have a drink and make yourselves at home. We're all good friends here.'

'Do you have any food?' Jared said, not caring that it might sound rude. 'Alex has been at the races all day and she's starved.'

'Food? Yeah. Biscuits and cheese and dips in the kitchen. Better get stoked up.' He grinned at Alex and went to pinch her bottom until she saw his intention and side-stepped neatly, avoiding it. 'It could be a long night. You'll need lots of energy later on.'

Alex glanced quickly at Jared and saw he was starting to look as anxious as she felt.

'Why's that?' she said. 'Are we going to be dancing?'

'Dancing? Isn't she a sweet, old-fashioned thing? Didn't I mention it, Jared? We're having a rainbow party tonight.'

'Really?' said Alex. 'I've always loved rainbows.'

'Jon?' a mournful female voice called from a

81

nearby room. She sounded as if she had a cold. 'Where are you? We're getting lonely here.'

'Duty calls.' Jon gave them a sly smile. 'Make yourselves at home and I'll see you later.'

'Much later,' Jared muttered. 'Change of plan, Alex. We're out of here. This sort of party isn't for us.'

Relief made Alex giggle nervously. 'I'm not going to argue with that.'

They tiptoed to the front door and slipped out, leaving it as they'd found it, slightly ajar. Then, holding hands and laughing madly, as if they were escaping from the mouth of Hell, they ran all the way back to the car.

'Alex, what can I say?' Jared said at last. He had been laughing so hard, it took him a moment or two to regain his breath. 'I went to school with Jon and we've known each other forever. He can be a bit wild, but I've never known him to host a party like that. He must've fallen in with a different crowd. I'm so sorry—so embarrassed.'

'Don't be. It was an experience, wasn't it? Jared, what is a rainbow party?'

'Believe me, Alex, you don't want to know.' He glanced at his watch. 'And you must be starving still. D'you want me to pull strings at one of our restaurants and take you to dinner?'

'Not really, no. D'you know what I'd really

82

like?'

'Name it. I owe you.'

'It's a lovely night and a shame to be indoors. So let's go to St Kilda. A place I know has absolutely the best fish and chips and we can eat them sitting on a bench by the sea. Then we can chat and really get to know one another.'

'Sounds good to me.'

Just over half an hour later, Alex and Jared were seated on a bench, overlooking the bay and devouring a generous helping of fish and chips.

'You can have fish and chips anywhere,' she said, 'but you can't beat watching the ocean and burning your mouth as you eat them sizzling out of the paper.'

Jared nodded his agreement, too busy eating to say any more. When they were done, they continued to sit there, watching the passing parade. Many people were out enjoying this balmy evening in late summer. Roller skaters and joggers passed by and people strolled on the beach holding hands, the whole scene illuminated by an enormous full moon. Jared went back to the café to purchase some cool drinks before reclaiming the seat beside her.

'So,' he said. 'Tell me all about Alex Hay. Horse whisperer extraordinaire.'

'Oh,' she groaned. 'How I wish Toby had never said that. It makes it so hard to live up to. Aside from that, there's nothing to tell, really.'

'Trying to get information from you is worse than drawing teeth.'

'That's because I don't like talking about myself or my uncomfortable family circumstances.'

'Uncomfortable?'

'Well, my dad's great—no complaints there. But I don't have a mum, I have a Mim—the classic stepmother figure. It was mutual hatred at first sight. And now it gets worse. My father's just told me she's having a baby and that'll take me out of the picture entirely. He used to call every week to see how I was doing but this new family will claim all his attention now. So, apart from my job with Magenta, I'm on my own. OK?' She hadn't meant to say so much or sound so bitter or emotional but this latest news had been festering in her for a week now and this was the first time she'd discussed it with anyone.

Jared nodded, surprisingly sympathetic. 'I can see why you're upset, but is it really so bad? It leaves you free and you're old enough to be your own woman now.'

'I haven't thought of it like that.'

Jared smiled and shrugged. She couldn't help thinking he saw things in very simple terms.

'Can we talk about something else? What about you? Weren't you supposed to be going to college?'

Jared pulled a face. 'I dropped out. Didn't see the point of wasting time with theory when I could be learning about my father's business at first hand on the shop floor. The restaurants more or less run themselves—it's the shipping line that interests me—import and export.' He fixed Alex with a look. 'I'm not a typical second son, you see. More like that new baby your father's getting now.'

'What do you mean?'

'It's like this. When Pop goes—not too soon, we hope—Grady will get the horse-racing side of the business—and the house that goes with it, of course. That's fine with me—I know nothing at all about horses and, apart from enjoying a day at the races, I couldn't care less. But I'm to inherit everything else.'

'Everything?' She thought about this for a moment. 'And what about Grady? Is he OK with that?'

'It's a done deal and he has no choice. Before she married the old man, my mother devised the pre-nup from hell. She made him promise—and put it in writing—that any child of her own should inherit the lion's share of his estate. My mother can be a dragon lady at times and she always gets what she wants.'

'Wow!' Alex said softly as she assimilated this new information. Although she was drawn to Jared, who made her weak with longing whenever she looked at him, she felt more than a pang of sorrow for Grady who appeared to be cheated out of a large part of his rightful inheritance.

'I can see you think it's unfair but the agreement was made twenty years ago when the stable was the largest part of his enterprise. His other businesses weren't nearly as substantial as they are now.' Jared stood up, rolled the remains of their dinner into a large, paper ball and bowled it overarm into a rubbish bin. Alex applauded.

'So, tell me about Grady.' She was finding out a lot about the workings of the Allen family and was interested to learn more. 'Why has he never married? Or maybe he has been?'

'Not he. Oh, there was some fuss about a girl a long time ago when he was young.'

'Come on, Jared, he isn't that old.'

'No? I think Grady was born old.'

'So what happened to this girl of his? Why didn't he marry her?'

'I don't know.' Jared pulled a wry face, bored with the subject of his older brother. 'Nobody's talked about it for years. I think she died.'

'That's terrible. Poor Grady. What did she die of?'

'Like I say—I don't know. It was years ago and I was only a kid. I think it was some kind of accident but everyone shut up about it around me.'

'And he's been alone ever since? He never

86

found anyone else?'

'Clearly not.' He laughed shortly. 'Or else he's dating the invisible woman.'

She stared at him for a moment. 'Why do you hate your brother, Jared?'

'That's rather a strong word.' He stared at her in surprise. 'Of course I don't hate him— why would you say that? He's just my older brother and we're very different, that's all.'

'No, Jared, there has to be more to it than that.'

'All right. He was always trying to keep me on the straight and narrow when I was a kid.'

'Yeah? What did you do that was so bad?'

'Nothing.' Jared was clearly uncomfortable with her questions. 'Just the things all kids do. Taking unscheduled days off school. Pinching magazines and sweets from the newsagent. Grady was always on my case like a personal minder—I couldn't get away with anything. Usually, he dealt with my crimes on his own but when he caught me with some ecstasy pills, he took me to Pa. I really did hate him for that one—I was grounded for weeks.'

'I should think so. Kids die from using that stuff.'

'Nah! It was probably made of lemon sherbert—not even the real thing.' He danced a few steps away and spun around in front of her. 'But I don't want to talk about Grady— it's boring when we're out on a date. What would you like to do now?'

Alex glanced at her watch. 'It's getting rather late—well, it is for me, anyway. And it'll take us at least an hour to get home.'

'In Pop's Mercedes? Wanna bet?'

'All right, I'll stay out as late as you want,' she said rashly. 'But you have to tell me what a rainbow party is. I've been wondering about it all night.'

'Oh, Alex, no.' He groaned.

'Otherwise I'll insist on going home now.' Mischievously, she added an afterthought just to test him— 'And I'll never go out with you again. Ever.' Although, she reminded herself, if he ran true to form, he was unlikely to ask.

He glanced around, as if wondering who might be listening in 'I'll have to whisper,' he said. 'I really can't talk about something like this out loud.'

He leaned forward, cupping his hand to her ear while Alex could scarcely concentrate on what he was saying because of his nearness and the warmth of his breath, tickling her ear. Her eyes widened as she realized what he was saying and she drew back to stare at him.

'But that's so disgusting. So gross. I had no idea.'

'Well, you insisted.' He shrugged. 'I did say you wouldn't want to know.'

'You're telling me girls actually compete to leave rings of different coloured lipstick on a guy's—?'

'Ssh!' Jared started to laugh again. 'We'll be

88

arrested for having an indecent conversation.'

'Can you be arrested for that?'

'I don't know but I don't want to stick around to find out.'

CHAPTER FIVE

The many events of the evening had served to break any ice and sweep away all the barriers between them until Alex found she was enjoying herself hugely. Jared had a ready wit, was quick to laugh and had the knack of making her feel as if she had known him forever. They went to a club nearby and danced for a while and then, although Alex was still having the time of her life, the long day began to catch up on her. The driving beat of the music was starting to give her a headache and she caught herself flagging and stifling yawns.

'I'm so sorry,' she said, 'but I really will have to call it a night. This particular Cinderella is used to being in bed before ten, let alone twelve.'

'OK.' Jared didn't argue; he could see that she was genuinely tired out. 'I know all about girls who look after horses.' Alex frowned, reminded at once of Katrina's warning—Jared had taken out nearly every girl in the stables and kept everyone at a distance afterwards by being a serial 'once only' dater.

But he was nothing if not considerate. Before driving home, he tucked a car rug around her knees, even though the night wasn't cold, making her smile sleepily at this small attention. Warm now and mesmerized by the purring sound of the powerful Mercedes eating up the highway, she was soon fast asleep, her head drooping more and more until at last it rested on Jared's shoulder. She didn't wake until she felt the car turn from the main road, taking the long drive that lead to the Allens' stables. Forcing herself from her slumbers as Jared cut the motor, allowing the car to coast to a stop outside the girls' dormitories, she groaned, realizing that she was going to get little more than an hour in bed before it was time to get up and start her morning routine with Magenta.

'Thank you so much for tonight, Jared,' she murmured as he handed her out of the car. 'I had a wonderful time.'

'So did I.' He responded, still wide awake. 'But do me a favour, please, and don't mention Jon's party to anyone—I'll never live it down.'

She giggled at the memory. 'Will he be very offended with you for leaving?'

'I doubt it. The state he was in, he won't even remember who was there and who wasn't.' Jared shrugged. 'Anyway, he should know better.' He leaned forward to give her a

90

chaste kiss on the forehead, hands free. 'Thank you for a most interesting and unusual evening, Alex. I hope we can do it again soon.'

'Do you?' she said. 'Really?' And, surprising herself as much as Jared, she moved in closer, linked her arms around his neck and gave him a long and searching kiss on the lips. Although he tensed, surprised by her taking the initiative, it was a wonderful first kiss, everything she had always hoped it would be.

'Oh, Alex,' he murmured, as he turned up the wattage, pulled her right in against his hips and returned the kiss with enthusiasm. She could feel his erection in a matter of seconds.

Aware that she had unthinkingly roused the tiger when she had been half asleep, Alex murmured 'G'night,' tore herself away from his embrace while she still could, removed her shoes to creep past Mrs Brookes's door and took the stairs two at a time, trying to make as little noise as possible. Everyone would have to be awake and at work in less than two hours.

Outside the room she shared with Katrina, she paused, seeing light under the door. At this late hour, all the lights should be out and her room mate asleep but she opened it to find Katrina sitting up in bed, waiting for her, looking anxious and upset.

'What is it?' Alex immediately thought the worst. 'Has something happened to Madge?

Why didn't you call me?'

'Oh dear, Alex.' Katrina's lips trembled; she seemed to be on the verge of tears.

'Just tell me that Madge is OK.'

'Madge is absolutely fine—now. But it's been such a terrible night.'

Realizing that Katrina was not to be bullied and would tell her story only in her own time, Alex perched herself in lotus position on the end of the other girl's bed, waiting for her to elaborate.

'I didn't go down to check on Madge until half past nine,' Katrina said.

'Why? I usually go between eight and half past?'

'I know that. But to be honest I was tired and nearly forgot. Anyway, it was just as well. Even before I got to her stall, I knew something was wrong. I sensed that she wasn't alone. She whinnies and gets kind of antsy when there's someone around who scares her.'

'Yeah. Go on.'

'I crept up to the stall without making a sound and saw Bob in there, keeping his distance from her of course, but he seemed to be messing about with what remained of her feed.'

Alex clapped a hand over her mouth. 'But nobody knows the right mix except Toby an' me. What did you do?'

'I didn't want to challenge him by myself— he can be a bully and I was scared. But when I got back outside, I ran up to the house and rang the bell, hoping Grady would answer it, rather than Mr or Mrs Allen. Mr Allen employed Bob in the first place and I knew he'd take a lot more convincing that there was anything wrong.'

'Yes, yes—go on.' Alex was almost vibrating with impatience.

'Fortunately, it was Grady who came to the door and he got the message immediately—I didn't have to go into detail. We arrived back at the stables just in time to see Bob sneaking out.

Grady asked him what he was doing there so late at night and he made up some story that he thought he'd heard an intruder and gone to investigate. And that might've worked too, if I hadn't already spotted him messing about with Magenta's feed. Hoping to cause trouble for you, I'd say.'

'But Grady didn't accept his explanation?'

'No. He made Bob turn out his pockets. And there it was. He didn't even have time to throw it away. A crumpled, empty packet of bicarb. If Madge had eaten it and it remained in her system, she would have been compromised for her race next week.'

'But can you be sure that she didn't?'

'Not entirely. But she seemed more interested in the hay bag you left for her. All the same, late as it was, Grady called the vet out to check on her. Far as the vet could tell, the horse was unharmed but she took blood samples as a precaution and the remains of the feed were sent to be analysed to make sure it was only bicarb and not something more sinister.'

'I should go down and see Madge now. Make sure she's OK. She gets upset so easily.'

'Don't do that. I've settled her and she's fine. You'll only stir everyone up if you go back at this time of night.'

'What will happen to Bob?'

'It's already happened. Grady sacked him on the spot and he may face criminal charges.'

'I hope so.' Alex could feel little sympathy, remembering the way Bob had teased the filly so cruelly before. 'He should be behind bars—banned from coming near any racing stables for life.'

'He will be, I'm sure. Um—and there's one more thing.' Katrina looked vaguely uneasy. 'Grady seemed just a little bit mad that you hadn't come home.'

'Why? He knew I was having a night off.'

Katrina shrugged. 'Just the impression I got.'

*   *   *

In the morning, the news travelled around the stables like wildfire. Katrina and Alex soon got tired of explaining Bob's absence and repeating the story to everyone. With Bob

94

gone, a new track rider would have to be found to replace him and there was wild speculation about this. Would one of the younger lads get promoted or would Grady want to bring in somebody new? Alex was ready to champion Mick, who had improved out of sight after breaking away from his toxic friendship with Bob, but she wasn't at all sure that Grady would take her advice.

Magenta appeared to have suffered no harm from the upset of last night but nothing would be certain until the results of her blood tests were known. Whatever happened, her campaign would have to be halted until she was given the all clear.

Mid morning, Grady summoned Alex to Toby's office. As she approached the open door, she was surprised by the sound of argument from within.

'With respect, sir,' this was from Toby, 'I do think you're being a little harsh.'

'I disagree. We adhere to very high standards here and I expect the staff to uphold them.'

Alex knocked, waiting to hear no more. Toby came past her on his way out and he gave her a shrug and a sympathetic smile.

'Sit down Alex,' Grady said, indicating the chair on the other side of his desk. He came to the point quickly without preamble as soon as the door closed behind Toby.

'Katrina must have told you what happened

last night?'

'Yes. Late as it was, I wanted to go and see Madge right away, but Kat said it would be best to wait until morning.'

'Yes. And if we'd all waited until morning, goodness knows what might have happened.'

'Everyone knew I was going out. That's why I asked Katrina to keep an eye on her. I had a feeling someone might take advantage when I wasn't there.'

'And you were right. But Madge is *your* responsibility, Alexis.' He stabbed an accusatory finger towards her. 'Not Katrina's. Remember what you signed up for when you came here—commitment to the horses, twenty-four seven.'

Alex stared at him. This was so unfair when he himself had invited her out for a meal.

'You knew I was going to a party with Jared. It wasn't exactly a secret.'

'That's right. But did you have to stay out until after two in the morning? Rather irresponsible when you have work the next day.'

Alex couldn't believe it. She was being reprimanded like a truanting schoolgirl.

'You are not my keeper, Mr Allen.'

'No, indeed. But you are Magenta's. Most of our strappers have at least two horses to care for if not three. You have it easy with just one.'

'Oh, I have it easy, do I?' Alex saw red and

stood up, placing her hands on the desk to confront him. 'It's all very well for you to say that now. Everyone knows Magenta's a special case. Most people were scared to death of her and wouldn't go near before I took over. But now I've tamed her sufficiently for any sensible person to handle, I'm dispensable, I suppose?'

Grady looked down his nose at her. 'No one is saying you haven't done a good job—a great job—the result we had yesterday was exceptional. But in many ways you are still very young—perhaps a little flighty—'

'Flighty?' Alex ground out the word. 'And what exactly do you mean by that?'

'From time to time you may need to be reminded of your duties here.'

'Since when have I ever neglected my duties? You surely can't hold me responsible for what happened last night. If Bob was doing this to get me in trouble, he could have done so at any time—even when I was here.'

She paced the room for a moment, thinking, and then paused to stare at Grady as if she'd just had a revelation.

'This isn't about Magenta at all, is it? Or me. It's not even about Bob. You're actually jealous of Jared, aren't you? Jealous that I stayed out so late spending time with your brother.'

'Don't be ridiculous,' Grady muttered. But an angry red was staining his cheeks, giving the lie to his words and he found it difficult to meet her gaze.

'Well, well.' She leaned forward, smiling, trying to get him to face her. 'The inscrutable Grady Allen has an Achilles heel and I found it.'

She realized she had gone too far when he seized her face in both hands and gave her a bruising kiss on the lips. It didn't last more than a moment and just as suddenly, he let her go. They broke apart, staring into each other's eyes and both breathing heavily. Alex wondered why she had ever thought of him as someone too old for her. But he was quick to crush any romantic thoughts she might entertain.

'Forget about that,' he said, his voice still gruff. 'It never happened. And if you mention it to anyone, I shall deny it. Strenuously.'

Alex licked her lips, still tingling after the violence of that kiss. 'I don't know what to think,' she said, deciding to keep it light. 'Would you call that harassment in the workplace, Grady?'

'I wouldn't call it anything,' he said, recovering fast. 'Because nothing happened.'

'Of course not.' She gave him a mischievous smile as she reached the door. 'Except that it did.'

*   *   *

The next time she saw Grady, he treated her with his customary distant politeness and she began to wonder if she had imagined the whole thing. But, brief as it was, it had been a passionate kiss, a disturbing kiss, and she couldn't help remembering that she'd enjoyed it. At the same time, she knew Grady had done it on the spur of the moment when he was angry and that it was unlikely to happen again.

As she went through her routine of work with Magenta, she thought a lot about the two very different brothers and her relationship to them, concluding at last that she didn't have one. Grady had acted on impulse and if Jared ran true to form, he was unlikely to want to see her again.

Magenta's blood tests were returned as normal and she was cleared to race again. This time she was to appear at Caulfield on a Saturday—her first city meeting. Alex wasn't entirely happy, protesting to Grady that the filly could do with another quiet country race day as she didn't think Madge was ready to face a city crowd, but he waved away her fears. She also wondered if the Allens would turn out in force again and if Jared was going to be there.

She had been disappointed but not surprised when weeks passed into months and he made no attempt to contact her. Certainly, pride wouldn't allow her to ask after him. Yet he had seemed so sincere; she'd been so sure that he wanted to see her again. But his continued silence must mean that he thought no more of her than any other girl. What an idiot she'd been to be taken in by his superficial charm. She did her best to dismiss the Allen brothers from her waking thoughts but, together or separately, they haunted her dreams whether she would or no.

*   *   *

Having slept only fitfully, the night before Magenta's first city race day, she was up early to groom the filly and prepare her for her journey to town. Although the weather was mild for this time of year, it was chilly in these early hours of the morning.

Just as she had succeeded in banishing Jared from her waking thoughts, he turned up in the stables while she was drawing fresh water for Madge. Although it was the middle of winter in Melbourne, leaving most people pale and wan, Jared looked like a surfie, his sun-bronzed skin bringing out the dark blue of his eyes and his short fair hair bleached blonder than ever. It made her all the more conscious that she herself was looking washed out and weary, her hair still wet from the shower she had taken to wake herself up. Although her heart was beating with an excited rhythm of its own, she greeted him coolly, muttering that he had come at the wrong time and she was too busy to talk to him now. He caught her by the arm, spinning her to face him.

'Alex, don't be like that. I thought we were friends. Didn't anyone mention that I've been away?'

'No. No one said anything and I certainly wasn't going to ask. If you were on holiday, you could at least have sent me a postcard. That's what friends do.'

'Well, it was a spur of the moment thing—not exactly a holiday—'

'So where did you get the sun tan? A health spa?'

'My mother has a flat on the Gold Coast. Usually, she takes her best friend to soak up a bit of Queensland sunshine but the woman's not well and Ma didn't want to go on her own, so—'

'It doesn't matter, Jared. You don't have to explain yourself to me.' She tried to dodge past him and return to Magenta's stall but he anticipated her move, blocking it.

'I think I do. Without meaning to, it seems I've offended you.'

'Why should I be offended, Jared?' Alex shrugged. 'I had my one date, same as everyone else. What have I to complain about?'

He frowned. 'And what do you mean by that?'

'Katrina told me. You have a reputation for

dating a girl once and then dumping her.'

'For a small girl, Katrina has a big mouth.'

'Look, Jared, I really don't have time to talk to you now. The float will be here for Madge at any moment and she isn't ready.'

'Then let me help you.'

'No, because you'll only upset her. You said yourself, you don't know your way around horses.'

'See you at the races, then. And keep tonight free. Win or lose, we're going out on the town.'

'No way. I got into serious trouble with Grady for staying out late the last time.'

'Don't take any notice of him. I'll square the old grouch.'

'Don't bother'—Alex turned her back on him—'because I'm not going out with you anyway.' She didn't see it but she could well imagine the look of astonishment on his face. This must the first time someone had rejected the great Jared Allen.

*   *   *

If Alex hadn't been distracted by Jared, she might have been more observant of Madge and seen that she wasn't entirely happy. The filly objected, like a spoilt child, to every move she was asked to make. And, as she was the only horse from the Allen stables booked to race at Caulfield that day, by the time the float arrived to collect her, it was already half full of horses from other stables. Madge whinnied and wouldn't go into her place in the float. She continued to refuse until the stable dog came and growled at her, jumping back just in time to avoid a vicious side kick to his head. Alex felt like kicking him herself for upsetting Madge further.

At this point, she realized it was going to be 'one of those days' and Madge might as well be scratched from the race now for all the good she would do. She looked around, hoping to see Grady and make him understand, but he was nowhere in sight. The man driving the float was tapping his foot, anxious to be on his way.

'Are you coming or not, missie?' He said to Alex, as he glanced at his watch. 'I've got two more pick-ups to make before we hit town.'

'No, I'm ready,' she murmured. 'Oh, but wait a moment, I nearly forgot the bag.' She dashed back to Magenta's stall where she had left it. It would be a disaster to arrive without all the nylon ropes, brushes and grooming bits and pieces the filly would need on race day. She threw the bag and herself aboard the float and they were on their way.

It wasn't a comfortable ride. Magenta kicked out at the narrow space that confined her and, more than once, the driver informed Alex that the Allens would have to pay for any damage to his float.

On arrival at Caulfield, Alex saw that Magenta was sweated up and in a high old temper. There was nothing she could do to tease her out of it. This time her race wasn't until three o'clock so Alex was hoping that a few hours of peace and quiet in the stables might calm her.

She was so concerned about Madge, she dared not leave her, even for a moment, feeling sure that Grady must come and see them before long. But he didn't. Half an hour before the race, Tasha Trussardi called by to see them.

'Lordy, Alex, what's wrong with her?' Tasha could see at once that the filly was nervous and all wasn't well.

'I don't know,' Alex said, herself close to tears. 'It's no good expecting Madge to race on form when she's in a mood like this, but there was no one to ask. If I'd seen Grady, I'd have urged him to scratch, but I haven't seen him. He hasn't been near us all day.'

'D'you want me to find him?'

Miserably, Alex shook her head. 'It's too late now, in any case. We'll just have to hope it won't end in disaster.'

'Come on, Alex. This isn't like you.' Tasha grinned. 'You know Madge. She'll be OK when she gets out there and the competitive spirit kicks in.'

'I hope you're right.' Alex managed a wan
104

smile.

Before the race, Magenta stalked around the mounting yard as if she owned it, but she was still sweating up as if she had finished a race instead of being about to run. Alex wiped a lot of it away but the filly sweated again just as readily.

Out on the track on the way to the barriers, she looked good and Tasha gave Alex a sneaky 'thumbs up' as they passed the winning post on the way out. But when they arrived at the starting gates, Magenta dug her hoofs into the ground and wouldn't go in.

'Come on, Madge!' Tasha tried to encourage her mount with her knees. 'You're not scared of this. We've done it a dozen times.' But the filly wouldn't budge and, before Tasha could warn him to keep clear, one of the barrier attendants seized Madge's bridle and tried to drag her into her appointed place. Madge lashed out without warning and the young man screamed and fell to the ground, clutching his knee and obviously in great pain. The paramedics left their ambulance and rushed to help him.

Satisfied to have drawn blood, Madge then allowed Tasha to guide her into the stall.

Perhaps, if all the horses had settled and the starter had been able to let them go quickly, all might yet have been well. But in the stall next to Magenta, a horse reared, ending up on the ground with his jockey standing up in the stalls. The race was held up while the barriers were opened to get him out and further delayed by the veterinary inspection to see if the animal was still fit to race.

More minutes passed and Madge decided she'd waited long enough. She burst through the front of her stall, dislodging Tasha on the way. Alex, who had remained downstairs rather than join the Allens up in the stands, could only look on in horror. She had seen the incident with the barrier attendant and could only hope that Madge wouldn't harm the clerk or his horse when they tried to capture her.

Relishing her freedom and believing she was running the race of her life, Madge evaded all attempts to catch her and the race was further delayed as she remained on the course. Having seen what had happened to the boy at the barriers, the clerk rode after her, knowing he must try to stop her but also nervous and wary of getting too close.

Alex knew she was the only one who might have a chance of catching the wayward filly and, as Madge passed the winning post, totally pleased with herself, Alex ran out on the track, hoping to put an end to the drama. Vaguely, she was also conscious that someone was following her. Grady.

Bewildered after 'winning' her race, Magenta faltered to a stop and Alex reached out for her reins which were now dangling perilously in front of her, threatening to trip her if she took off again. But Magenta wasn't done yet. Furious at the thought of recapture and too upset by the day's events to recognize anyone, let alone her regular handler, quick as a snake, she moved her head and sank her teeth into Alex's slender forearm. Alex screamed in pain and fell to her knees as blood poured from her wrist; it felt as if her hand were being cut off. Vaguely, she was aware that Grady had taken command, seizing the horse with the clerk supporting him on the other side, placing his own horse in such a way to prevent Magenta's escape. Always squeamish at the sight of blood, particularly her own, Alex took one look at her mangled wrist and, mercifully, lost consciousness.

*   *   *

She knew no more until she came to in a hospital bed, recognizing her father at her bedside. Vaguely, she had been aware of a dash to hospital in an ambulance and people talking around her as she was wheeled along on a trolley under bright overhead lights.

'Dad?' She said, still feeling muzzy and trying to sit up. Gently, Vere pushed her back on to the pillows.

'Take it steady, Alex,' he said. 'Magenta severed an artery and you've lost a lot of blood. You're going to need microsurgery to mend it tomorrow morning, so they're

107

keeping you in here overnight.'

'An operation?' Alex groaned. 'Oh, no. But how is Magenta, Dad? She only bit me because she was frightened. Is she safe?'

'Safe as she'll ever be.' Vere muttered. 'She'll be cat's meat after this.'

'No! No, please, it's not fair. I don't want her punished for this. It wasn't her fault—'

'It's not just you, Alex. She smashed that boy's knee, remember?'

'Please, Dad, you must help me get up.' Alex swung her legs off the bed where she paused, overtaken by vertigo yet again. She realized, at the same time, there were tubes and drips attached to her arm, restricting her movements. She would have to stay where she was.

'Calm down, Alex. You aren't anywhere near as strong as you think.'

'I don't care about me, but I have to see Grady. Stop him from doing this.'

'All right. Just stay where you are and I'll fetch him. He's outside waiting to see you. So's Jared.'

'Both of them?'

'Oh yeah.' Vere smiled at her. 'What kind of spell have you cast on those boys, hon?'

'Nothing.' She blushed at his teasing. 'They're very competitive with each other, that's all.'

'So I see. Which one do you want to see first?'

'Grady, of course. I have to persuade him not to let anyone hurt Madge.'

CHAPTER SIX

Vere returned very quickly with Grady. Jared peered into the room and attempted to follow them but a nurse stopped him, saying that Alex was not to have more than two visitors at a time and must not be overtaxed or excited.

'Grady, how is Magenta?' she asked at once, dispensing with any greeting. 'Please don't tell me you've let anyone hurt her?'

'Not yet.' Grady sighed, glancing at Vere to avoid the intensity of her stare. 'Alex, I hate to tell you this when I know you feel you have a special bond with this filly—'

'I do, Grady. You know I do.'

'But, after today's performance, there's no other course open to us. This experiment has to be over—'

'No. Listen to me, please. It wasn't her fault. I told you she wasn't ready to face the crowds and when that horse reared in the barrier next to her, she just took fright.'

'But that happens all the time—you know it does. Horses rear in the barriers almost every race day.' Grady spoke softly but firmly. 'There's no such thing as a perfect start with young horses. Let it go, Alex. Enough is enough. Just as I feared, she's put you in hospital along with that other young man who faces a long time in rehab, even if they can repair his knee. And on top of that, we're getting a big bill for the damage she did to the float.'

'I see.' Alex fought to hang on to her anger rather than burst into tears. 'So it's all down to money now, is it?'

'With my father, it always has been. He's furious, of course, as well as enjoying himself and saying *I told you so*. He refuses to let me bring Magenta back home.'

'So where is she?' Alex struggled to sit up as Grady stood by the bed silent, not knowing what he could say to make it right. 'What will happen to her now?'

'I asked Toby to come up from Cranbourne with a horse box to collect her and deliver her to—to the yards.'

'Where they'll kill her?'

'Alex,' Vere broke in. 'You must calm down or the nurses will send us away. Your blood pressure must be sky high and it's doing you no good to get so upset.'

'How can I be calm till I know Magenta is safe? Please, Dad, will you take her to your place until I can get out of here and have time to decide what to do? I can't let them murder my horse.'

'But Alex,' her father said gently, 'she isn't your horse—'

'Please, Grady.' Alex clutched his arm with her one good hand and hung on for dear life. 'Please make that phone call to Toby before it's too late.'

'OK,' Grady said at last. 'If it means that much to you, Alex. Maybe we all need to slow down and think it through rather than respond with a knee-jerk reaction.'

'And you, Dad?' Alex was still waiting for her father's response. He was still looking far from happy.

'She can stay for a night or two—'long as she doesn't cause any more trouble.' Vere said at last. 'I sold a few horses last week so our stables are half empty at present. That'll give Grady a chance to talk to his father and decide what is best for everyone.'

'Oh, thank you.' Alex fell back against her pillows, weak with relief.

'This is just a reprieve, mind. And you must promise to abide by whatever the Allens decide?'

'Yes, yes of course.' Alex felt sure that with time on her side, she could convince Grady to take Madge home and give her a second chance. He wouldn't admit it right now but she knew he was just as devoted to the difficult filly as she was. 'But please, hurry now and make that phone call to Toby before he gets on his way.'

'I still don't know what my father will say.'

'I'll talk to Mr Allen.' Having won this small

111

victory, Alex was convinced that she could move mountains now.

'You will, will you?' Grady gave a wry smile. All the same, he hurried outside to switch on his mobile and talk to Toby. While he was doing this, Jared slipped into the room.

'Hello, it's Toby.' The foreman answered promptly although he seemed to have lost his usual bounce. 'Yes, Grady, I've collected Magenta an' I'm on my way. Although I have to say I've been draggin' me feet. That lovely animal—so full of life and vigour—it seems such a shame.'

'Change of plan, Toby,' Grady said crisply. 'You'll be pleased to hear we're thinking along the same lines—although if she shows up at our place at any time soon, my father will have a pink fit.'

'What's to do then?' Toby brightened considerably.

'You can drop her over to Belvedere Hay's place at Wonga Park. D'you know where that is?'

'Sure do. Collected you from there often enough when you were a lad.'

'Yes, well. Vere's agreed to hang on to her for a night or so until we decide what to do.'

'Good man. I really wasn't looking forward to dropping her off at the yards.'

'We're not out of the woods yet— particularly where the old man's concerned— but let's take it one day at a time, eh?' He

112

switched his phone off and returned to report the good news to Alex, giving her the thumbs up through the little window in the door of her room. Vere stood up and kissed his daughter, leaving so that Grady could come in. Vere promised to come back and give her his support in the morning but now he needed to get home quickly to meet Toby and help him to settle Magenta into her new quarters.

Grady came into the room to find Jared sitting beside Alex's bed, clutching her uninjured hand and kissing it; the other one was in a bandage and splint to hold it secure until she had surgery in the morning. Somehow the sight of his brother playing the lover filled him with impatience and irritation.

'Seeing you hurt was one of the worst moments of my life.' Jared was saying. 'Are you sure you're OK?'

'Of course she isn't OK.' Grady said, scowling at his brother. 'And be careful with her, will you?—she's probably still in pain.'

'Ooh, sorry.' Jared winced, at once letting go of her hand.

With a reproachful look at Grady, Alex linked hands with Jared again. 'I don't mind,' she smiled, looking up at him. 'I'm not in pain at all now and I like holding your hand.'

'Well, I can see I'm superfluous to requirements here,' Grady muttered. 'I'll get on home and set about calming the elderly lion in his den.'

'Thanks, Bro,' Jared said automatically without looking up. All his attention was centred on Alex.

Momentarily, she tore herself away from the younger man's mesmerizing gaze. 'I owe you, Grady. Thank you so much for saving Magenta for me. You're my white knight.'

Grady huffed, unsure how to take the compliment and shaking his head. 'It's only a stay of execution, Alex. You know it could still end in tears.'

'I refuse to believe it. Not with Grady Allen in charge.'

'My brother is such a bear,' Jared murmured, when Grady was out of earshot. 'Someone should teach him how to accept a compliment.'

'I won't hear a word said against him,' Alex cried. 'Not today.'

Jared stayed, holding Alex's hand and smoothing her hair away from her face until her eyes closed and she let herself drift into sleep.

*   *   *

Alex's microsurgery was successfully carried out the next day but her hand and wrist would have to remain in a cast for some weeks. She wasn't allowed to leave the hospital until she was fully recovered from the anaesthetic and, for the first time in a while, she was actually

114

looking forward to returning to her old home at Wonga Park. She tried not to look too jubilant when Vere told her Mim wouldn't be there. She was away in Sydney, visiting her mother and escaping the worst of the Melbourne winter. Pregnancy didn't agree with her, Vere said. It made her feel sick and shivery and she was looking forward to being pampered by her mother who was in seventh heaven anticipating the arrival of the grandchild she never expected to have. Mim had only just left and wasn't likely to return for at least six weeks.

'I must see Madge first and make sure she's OK.' Alex scrambled out of the Mercedes as soon as it stopped outside the house.

'Give yourself a chance, Alex. You're still weak from surgery and an anaesthetic. Magenta's OK. She's stabled next door to old Hotspur, Toby left full instructions about her feed and I've set my best girl to look after her.'

'I know all that, Dad. But I won't rest easy until I've seen her.'

'I'll come with you, then.'

A very different Magenta greeted them from the angry, frightened horse she had been at the track. She whinnied softly at Alex and nuzzled her, almost as if she were apologizing for the terrible injury she had inflicted upon her handler the previous day.

'You've been a very naughty girl,' Alex said,

stroking her nose. 'And I still don't know how we'll persuade Mr Allen to have you back.'

The filly snickered as if she were laughing. Hal Hotspur in the stall next to her whinnied in response.

'Oh no, missie,' Vere said. 'You needn't think you've found a permanent berth here even if old Hotspur thinks he's in love with you. I've no room for a renegade racehorse disturbing my show ponies.'

'But, Dad'—Alex stared at him, biting her lip—'what am I going to do if Morris refuses to have her back?'

Although her father had no ready answer for this question, it was to be answered decisively within the next twenty-four hours. Morris Allen, who had always claimed rude health, dismissing his doctor's recommendations and refusing to recognize that he had high blood pressure as well as cholesterol problems, suffered a massive heart attack followed by a stroke. He had been taken to hospital where the doctors warned the family to prepare for the worst. Even if Morris could make a partial recovery, he would never be the same as before.

Having expected their irascible parent to remain in command of his business empire for at least another decade, both Grady and Jared were stunned, not least by the responsibilities that must now fall on them, much earlier than they had expected.

116

'I did love him, Bro.' Jared said, weeping unashamedly, as they sat hunched before a huge open fire which didn't seem able to warm them. 'But I never found the right time to say so.'

'And, knowing him, he wouldn't have let you.' Grady sighed, wishing he had his younger brother's lack of inhibition and ability to show his emotions so freely. Instead, he felt incredibly sad and empty as well as partly responsible for his father's illness. It all came back to his own stubbornness over that horse. He had been so determined to prove himself right. But then, he reminded himself, if not Magenta, there would have been some other drama or crisis to hasten his father's demise.

When Morris fell ill, Simone had become hysterical and took to her bed, leaving Grady to deal with everything. He summoned an ambulance that arrived promptly and took his father to the private hospital he favoured. The paramedics said that Morris would remain unconscious for some time so there was little point in accompanying them. Grady tried to call Jared only to find his mobile seemed to be switched off. He then waited up for his brother who didn't return until the early hours of the morning. Having switched off his mobile at the hospital the previous day, typically, he had forgotten to turn it on again or recharge it.

Grady now stared at his younger brother,

thinking he seemed scarcely more than a schoolboy; someone who couldn't even remember to recharge a mobile phone. Even with experienced business people to advise and guide him, he was very young to receive control of the complicated structure that was their father's business empire. He would have no such problems with his own legacy; he knew what he needed to do to improve the stables and his strike rate as a trainer, especially if he was no longer hampered by Morris's caution. At the same time he felt guilty for looking forward to having a free hand while his father was still alive.

Idly, he also wondered what Jared's mother would do. As a rule, Simone fled from her husband's temper or dealt with any crisis in her life by running away to her refuge on the Gold Coast. This time, she wouldn't be able to do so; not with Morris in hospital, hovering on the brink of death.

*   *   *

Alex knew nothing of this until the following day although she did wonder if Grady had had the chance to broach the subject of Magenta with his father and what the outcome might be. The filly had settled in her new quarters surprisingly well but she was restless and already missing her exercise sessions with Tasha Trussardi. Alex wasn't yet well enough even to walk her and, although Magenta was much better behaved towards men, she wasn't prepared to risk her with anyone else.

In the event it was Jared rather than Grady who drove up to Wonga Park to let them know what had happened to Morris. Vere was away in town and Alex greeted him at home alone, shocked when she saw his pallor and the purple smudges underneath his eyes. He looked crushed; totally unlike the carefree young man he had been a few days ago. She led him into the kitchen, bracing herself for bad news about Magenta although, at the same time, she wondered why Jared, who had nothing to do with the work of the stables, should be so upset.

'You'd better sit down.' She indicated a chair at the kitchen table. 'You look terrible, Jared.'

'Thanks.' He gave a wry smile. 'You really know how to cheer a man. Does Vere keep any whiskey?'

She searched the cupboards and found a half bottle of Irish, setting it in front of him with a glass and bracing herself to hear the worst. While she was waiting for him to speak, he poured himself a generous measure and tossed it back, replacing it at once with another.

'Bad news then, is it?' She prompted him. 'About Magenta?'

He blinked at her for a moment as if she

were speaking a foreign language. 'Magenta? God! Can't you think of anything except that blasted horse?'

Alex recoiled, shocked as if he had struck her. 'I'm sorry—but I thought that's why you were here—'

'No, no, I'm sorry. It's me. You're only just home from hospital and don't know what's been going on.' He looked shattered and seemed perilously close to tears, quite unlike the confident, rather brash young man she had known before.

'Just tell me what's happened, Jared. Surely, it can't be that bad.' She sat beside him, stroking his shoulder with her good hand.

'Oh yes, it is.' He closed his eyes and took a deep breath to compose himself. Gradually, he was able to tell her what had happened to his father, including that he had never recovered consciousness and died in the early hours of that morning.

'Everyone keeps saying it's for the best and I hate that. I expect it's all over the television news already.'

'I wouldn't know. I don't watch day time TV.'

'God, I hate those people. They're vultures. I wish they'd just leave us in peace.'

'They will. Soon as there's some other story to replace it.'

Jared sighed. 'And you know the worst thing is that I took Pa completely for granted.

120

Because he had always been there, I felt he'd be a part of my life forever. And now—now he's gone and I don't know what to do.'

'You're probably still in shock. How's your mother?'

'Hysterical and sedated. It's hard to know how she really feels. She relied on Morris for everything so I expect she's scared.'

'And Grady?'

'Oh, you know Grady. Stoic as ever. Seems to take everything in his stride.'

Alex didn't think so. Because Grady was good at concealing his feelings, Jared found it easy to dismiss them.

'You'd better stay and have supper with us,' she said at last. 'Having seen off most of that whiskey, you're in no fit state to drive.'

'No, I'm not.' Jared squinted at the almost empty bottle. 'Tell Vere I'll replace it.'

'No need. He prefers single malt anyway.'

'I'll get him that, then.' He glanced at her hand, still encased in a blue cast. 'And, out of interest, how are you going to make supper with one hand?'

'Easy,' she said. 'You can pull a salmon pie out of the freezer for me. Mim doesn't like fish, so there should still be one there.' She stood up and led the way to the pantry to show him where the freezer was.

While they were both in that confined space, Jared surprised her by catching her in his arms and kissing her. He didn't rush her, letting the

121

excitement build by taking it slow but nor did he give her the chance to break free. One kiss finished only to lead into another, still more demanding than the last. At last they came up for air and he smiled, gazing into her eyes and pushing his hand up under her sweater to feel her breast, making her gasp.

'You're pretty helpless, aren't you? With one hand in a cast,' he whispered, his lips very close to her ear. This was more like the cheeky Jared she knew.

'Not so.' She turned in his embrace to look at his lips. 'I could always beat you to death with it.'

'Bloodthirsty little wretch.' He grinned and then smothered her with yet another kiss. 'We fit so well together,' he said at last. 'You'll have to marry me, Alex.'

'What? What did you say?' She thought she must be hallucinating.

'I'm saying that we should be married. And you should be flattered. I've never thought about marrying anyone else before.'

'But why? What's so special about me?'

'Is it possible that you don't know how gorgeous you are? I love you, Alex Hay, and you're going to marry me.'

'No, Jared. I do like kissing you and I might even be a little in love with you—'

'Only a little?'

'But, of course, I can't marry you! I'm only eighteen and not ready to marry anyone.' She couldn't say so, of course, but an image of Grady had risen between them, along with the memory of that brief but unsettling kiss in Toby's office. 'Look, you're in emotional limbo, still grieving for your father—you've not even buried him yet. And you're in shock.'

'I know. And I am—all of that. But I want to bring some stability into my life.'

'Then surely your mother—'

He laughed without humour. 'My mother? You've seen her, haven't you? Much as I love her, my mother is a shallow bitch. Right now, she's probably lying in bed considering her options and deciding who's going to be her next husband.' He paused, shaking his head. 'And with the wrong person, I'd be just like she is. The bad genes are all there.'

Alex stared at him, not knowing what to say.

'You can't believe that, can you? You who are always so loyal and honest in your dealings with everyone, devoted even to that bloody horse when she tried to kill you.'

'Well, she didn't, did she? And don't call her "that bloody horse".'

'Alex, I've been in love with you from the moment I saw you at your birthday party—'

'Which was what? Less than a year ago. And you've been away so often I've hardly seen you. Kicking up your heels in Queensland with girls in mini-bikinis, no doubt.'

'No. I promise you, my heels stayed very firmly on the ground. I was thinking about you all the time'

'You didn't even send me a postcard.'

'You won't let go of that, will you?'

'And it's not as if we live in each other's pockets.'

'So? We get on famously when we are together. Promise me that you'll think about it, Alex. You love me more than a little—I know you do.'

There was no time for any further discussion along these lines as Vere arrived home, apologizing for being late and welcoming Jared as well as offering his sympathies. He had been listening to the radio on the way home and had already learned of Morris's death.

*   *   *

Although the brothers would have preferred a quiet family funeral, Simone wanted everyone to witness her grief, demanding something on the scale of a State funeral. Having married her husband in a civil ceremony and never having discussed his religion or his beliefs, she fell back on what had once been her own. As a lapsed Catholic, glossing over the fact that her marriage had not taken place in church, she convinced the priest that she wanted to re-enter the fold, arranging for the funeral to be held at the largest Catholic church in the district. She published extravagant notices in the local papers and, instead of a hearse, insisted that the coffin must arrive in a glass-sided Victorian funeral carriage drawn by a pair of black horses with black ostrich-feather plumes on their heads. And, while Grady and her son appeared in plain black suits and black ties, she arrived in swathes of black lace with an enormous hat and a veil to conceal her face; widow's weeds that would have done justice to Queen Victoria.

She wept noisily throughout the lengthy funeral service, attended by various personalities from the racing industry and many of her husband's employees. Fortunately, as it was a bitterly cold day and with intermittent rain, most people chose to leave after the service, leaving only family and close friends to attend the actual burial ceremony in the graveyard.

Vere and Alex, who had arrived late, stood at the back of the church for the service. Vere spoke briefly to Jared afterwards, hoping to escape and leave before the family left for the cemetery. Simone, looking pale and fragile, was almost collapsed in the arms of her best friend and Grady was shaking hands and farewelling others, thanking them for turning out on such a bleak winter's day.

'But you can't leave now,' Jared said, making Alex feel she had never seen him looking more vulnerable and needy. 'There's still the graveyard and the reception afterwards at the house. I can't get through it all without you.'

'But don't you think your mother would like some privacy?' Vere said gently, nodding towards Simone who was making a spectacle of herself, giving way to a new storm of tears.

'I don't think she knows the meaning of the word,' Jared said, not without bitterness. 'She can make a circus out of anything—even this.'

After that, there was no getting out of it. Vere and Alex were carried along to the ceremony at the graveyard and invited to join the small party afterwards at the house. Alex, who had been made uneasy rather than comforted by the Latin words and almost medieval ceremony, felt a sense of relief that the deceased had been finally buried and it was all over. Still tearful, Simone begged to be excused as, with her friend's arm still around her, she allowed herself to be guided upstairs.

Grady joined them soon after, pressing drinks into their hands. 'Thanks for coming,' he said. 'Not easy in this dirty weather. And thanks again for keeping Magenta for me, Vere. We'll keep it low profile, but I'll send Toby with the horse box to fetch her back home tomorrow.'

Vere nodded. 'Been a pleasure. Old Hotspur will miss her.'

'Oh, have they bonded?' Grady brightened considerably. 'Maybe you'd consider selling him to me? A companion horse can be very calming.'

'No, you can't have my Hotspur.' Vere grinned. 'He's earned his retirement and anyway, he's my pet.'

At that moment, although everyone thought they had seen the last of Simone for that day, she reappeared. Freshly made up and wearing an expensive, figure-hugging black jersey dress she seemed, for the moment at least, to have gained control of her emotions.

'Jared, darling,' she called to her son across the room, 'get me a gin and tonic, will you—a strong one.'

He measured the drink and passed it to her, saying nothing. Then he went to fetch Alex who was still talking to Grady and her father. 'Sorry to break up the party, guys. Need to borrow Alex for a moment.'

To Alex's surprise, he led her over to his mother.

'I'm so pleased to see you're feeling better, Mrs Allen—' Alex began, realizing she'd said the wrong thing when Simone flinched and her eyes filled with tears yet again.

'Better?' the woman whispered, pressing a lace handkerchief to her nose. 'I've lost my husband—my soul mate. I shall never be better—not in this lifetime.'

'Oh, Ma, cut the dramatics for just a moment, can't you?' Jared muttered. 'I've got something important to tell you.' He caught hold of Alex's good hand and wouldn't let go.

Simone closed her eyes and clasped her hands under her chin. 'Heartless boy! How can you think of anything but your father at a time like this?'

'He's gone, Ma, and we have to face up to it. No use dwelling on what can't be helped. We have to look to the future now.'

Simone opened her eyes and sighed. 'So where is this leading, Jared?'

'I want you to be the first to know. Alex is going to marry me and I'm hoping you'll wish us well and be happy for us.'

'Happy for you! Happy!' Simone's voice had risen to such a pitch that she silenced the room. Everyone stopped talking to see what was upsetting the widow now. Vere turned an enquiring gaze on his daughter who gave him a small frown, shaking her head. 'You're a boy—scarce into your twenties—too young to be married to anyone.'

Grady also had grown very still. 'Bad timing, Bro,' he muttered.

'This is outrageous.' Nostrils flaring, Simone turned cold fury on Alex. 'Taking advantage of my son when he's at his most vulnerable and bereaved.'

'Mrs Allen.' Alex was shaking; she hated scenes but felt bound to defend herself. 'I haven't taken advantage of anyone. I had no idea.' She wanted to say that she hadn't agreed to anything yet but, having worked herself into a temper, Simone didn't give her

128

the chance.

'Get out of my house now.' She pointed dramatically towards the door. 'I don't want you here.'

'Mother!' Jared was desperately trying to get her attention. 'If you'll just listen for a moment—'

'I'll deal with you later.' Simone ground out the words. Jared stared at her for a long moment and then strode from the room, slamming the door behind him.

This seemed to be the signal for everyone who wasn't close family to leave. They crowded towards the door, murmuring thanks for the hospitality to no one in particular and promising to keep in touch. Grady followed, shaking hands with the men and farewelling elderly ladies who presented withered cheeks to be kissed.

Vere moved with them, ushering Alex before him, until Grady surprised him by asking them both to wait.

'Wouldn't it be better if we left?' He nodded towards Simone. 'Red rag to a bull and all that?'

Grady smiled, waiting until there were just the four of them—himself, Alex, her father and Simone.

'Trust you and Jared to ruin a good party,' she murmured.

'This isn't a party, Simone.' For the first time Grady seemed likely to give way to

129

exasperation. 'It's the day of my father's funeral.'

'And no time for your brother to be speaking of marriage.' She pursed her lips and glowered at Alex.

'No and I have to agree with you there. Let's all sit down, shall we?' Grady indicated the massive L-shaped couch which would accommodate all of them. He poured whiskey shots for himself and Vere, refreshed Simone's gin and tonic and offered wine to Alex but she shook her head.

'Simone,' he said at last. 'I can't let you throw Alex out because she's my employee—and a valuable one.'

'Even if she's using her wiles to seduce your brother?'

Grady laughed. 'I don't think Alex has been seducing anyone. You shouldn't judge all women by your own actions, Simone.'

'Are you trying to insult me?'

'No but if the cap fits... Look, Simone, I know this isn't the ideal time when emotions are running high but, according to the terms of my father's will, this is my house now and it's up to me to say who is welcome here and who isn't.'

Simone resorted to tears again, sniffling into her sodden handkerchief.

'But—what am I going to do? This is my home.'

'Is it? How many weeks have you spent here

over the last year? Less than six months, I'm sure. Your real home is where you spend most of your time—your apartment in Surfer's—'

'But that's just a beach house. A holiday home.'

'I think it's a lot more than that.' Grady had to smile, thinking of the two huge bedrooms, each with an en-suite, as well as the enormous deck and patio with its double glazing attached to the lounge. Morris had also installed a top of the range galley kitchen although Simone rarely used it. There was also a private swimming pool, maintained for the use of residents. It was far from being a 'granny flat'.

'You can't turn me out of my home. I was Morris's wife.'

'Yes, indeed, but I am his eldest son and my father's wishes have always been clear on this. While you and Jared are to get everything else, I inherit the horses and the racing stables along with this house. I'm the one with the trainer's licence, after all.'

'You shan't get away with this, Grady. I'll contest it.'

'Think very carefully before you do. Lawyers are always an expensive option. My father has been more than generous. Presently, you have a large enough allowance to ensure that you'll never work again.'

'Work?' Simone made it sound like a dirty word. 'I've never had to work in the whole of my life.'

'Well'—Grady shook his head—'engage lawyers to fight me and all that could change. Such people are notorious for running away with the profits. It will benefit neither of us.'

'All right. What about Jared? Are you turning him out as well?'

Grady closed his eyes, shaking his head. 'Nobody's going to be turned out. Jared can stay here as long as he likes. But, ultimately, if he's taking control of Pa's business interests, he'll need an apartment in town.'

Alex frowned, biting her lip. She hadn't taken Jared's proposal seriously, believing it to have sprung from grief. But if she *did* marry him, it would mean she must move into town. And she was a country girl at heart, always had been.

Simone picked up on what Grady was saying. 'I see. So Jared is welcome to stay here as long as he likes and I'm not?'

'Simone, I never wanted to get into this—not today. But you were the one who brought up the subject of contesting Pa's very fair arrangements.'

Vere stood up. 'This is family business, Grady. I don't think we should be here, listening in. Come along, Alex.'

'No, Dad, I'm going to stay. In my old quarters with Katrina. Magenta will be coming back home tomorrow and I want to be here for her.'

'You and that filly,' Vere said, shaking his head. But he didn't argue further.

CHAPTER SEVEN

Back in her quarters with Katrina and returning to the daily routine of looking after Magenta, if only one-handed and with help from Toby and Mike, Alex felt as if the brief interlude with her father had scarcely taken place. Tasha Trussardi started training with Madge again and, although Grady was overseeing most of her work, he was prepared to be guided by Alex and enter her for a few low profile provincial races rather than hasten her return to a course in town. The cast came off Alex's wrist and she was allowed to exercise it although she was warned to take care as the damaged muscles would take some time to reach full strength.

Weeks passed and Jared stayed away, making her think his extravagant offer of marriage had been made on the spur of the moment and in a time of grief. She would have been foolish indeed to take him too seriously when he set the cat among the pigeons on the day of Morris's funeral. In some ways, she wasn't entirely sorry. Simone would make a formidable mother-in-law who had much higher aspirations for her beloved only son. She would have no wish to see him married to Alex who had little prospect of inheriting anything. And Jared, having second thoughts and regretting his impulsive offer, was wisely keeping out of her way until all memory of it had been forgotten.

Her own feelings remained ambivalent. She couldn't be sure if she was in love with him or not and found she was amused rather than heartbroken when he stayed away. Oh yes, there were times of physical longing, when she yearned for him to return and sweep away all her doubts with his kisses. Then at other times she remembered that rare moment of honesty—when he told her he had the potential to be as shallow and self-centred as his mother. Maybe that was the only time he had ever been honest and told her the truth. Occasionally, she let herself drift into a daydream about Grady but, since that brief and disturbing kiss, he had been distant, favouring her no more than any other member of staff. He spoke to her only in the presence of Toby or others and always about Magenta and any changes to her daily routine. He had never asked her to join him for dinner again and she didn't expect it. After all, as her father's friend, he must think of her as a child.

Speculation was rife in the stables when the lads saw a large interstate truck parked outside the house and men running to and fro carrying out furniture and luggage. Alex

134

called into Toby's office to find out what was going on.

'Mrs Allen is leaving,' he told her. 'Lucky for us it's a draughty old winter down here. She's finally been persuaded to take up residence on the Gold Coast. Grady's trying not to look too pleased.'

'And Jared?' Alex scarcely dared to ask. 'Is he going with her?'

'I should think not. He's got far too much to do here, coming to grips with his father's business in town. A lot of responsibility fell on young shoulders when the old man died. Too much, if you was to ask me.'

'But surely, Grady—?'

'Won't interfere. Or can't. Old Morris's will left everything very clear. Grady inherits the house, the stables and all of the horses his father owned. Jared gets everything else.'

'That doesn't seem fair.'

'Well, that's the way the old man left it. I hear Jared's already spending money like a man with no arms—new car and bought himself a big place in Docklands overlooking the marina. It's only a couple of years old but he's renovating throughout. Once he's settled in, I don't suppose we'll see too much of him here.'

'No.' Alex absorbed this information thoughtfully.

One chilly morning towards the end of August, as Alex was singing quietly to herself

135

as she groomed Magenta after her morning work-out, she heard someone give a piercing whistle just outside the door. The filly stamped and flinched, setting her ears back. She didn't relish such surprises.

'Hold the noise out there, will you?' Alex was irritated that anyone who knew the filly's temperament could be so inconsiderate. 'You're upsetting my horse.'

'Horse must get used to a lot more than that at the track,' said a voice she recognized. Getting ready to do battle, she went to the door to greet him, hands on hips.

'Jared. I might've known it was you,' she said, determined not to show she was pleased to see him. After causing mayhem by proposing to her at his father's funeral, he had disappeared without any explanation and she had every right to be angry. Even so, she knew her eyes would be glowing as her treacherous heart stepped up its beat.

He grinned. 'How's my best girl? Oh? Just as I remember her—with dirt on her face and reeking of horse shit.'

'Well, nobody asked you to come in here.' She tossed her head and stood squarely in front of him, meeting his gaze. 'And now I've had time to think about it, I might not want to be your girl, at all. Really, Jared, it's a good thing I don't take you seriously.'

He infuriated her by being amused. 'Oh darling, lovely Alex, don't you know how

136

beautiful you are when you're cross? Take me seriously, please.'

'That's all very well but what about your mother?'

'Forget my mother—she's a thousand miles from here and I'm now in the business of pleasing myself.' So saying, he revealed an extravagant bunch of flowers that he had been hiding behind his back. He made a small bow, presenting it to her with a flourish. It was a massive concoction of irises and liliums mixed with stems of bright blue delphiniums. Against her will, Alex caught herself blushing with pleasure as she held it in her arms and breathed in the exotic mixture of floral scents.

'How could I resist them?' Jared said. 'Iris and delphinium to match your pretty eyes.'

She opened them to stare at him, wondering how he could have made such a basic mistake. 'But, Jared, my eyes are brown, not blue.'

'Of course they are,' he said without missing a beat. 'I just wanted to see if you were paying attention.'

She couldn't help laughing at his nonsense, shaking her head. He was a subtle rogue but it was impossible not to be charmed by him. But Magenta, becoming annoyed that she no longer had her strapper's full attention, snorted and set her ears back, stamping her foot.

'Oh-oh,' Jared moved quickly out of her way. 'If madame's getting ready to have a tanty, I'm out of here. I'll call for you around eight tonight. We're going out for dinner and this time it's going to be more than fish and chips.'

'No way, Jared. I have to be up at dawn. Madge is booked to race in Cranbourne tomorrow. It's the first time she's been to the track since that disaster in the city. I can't afford to be tired.'

'Oh, you are so boringly conscientious. As bad as Grady with your devotion to that wretched horse. Tomorrow night then, after the races?'

'Jared, what makes you think I want to go out with you at all? You disappear for weeks, ignoring me—and not for the first time. Then you turn up here with a bunch of flowers, expecting me to fall into your arms.'

'It would be nice if you did but I didn't expect it.' He resorted to one of his favourite expressions, 'little boy lost'. 'I've had rather a lot on my plate, you know, since Pa died. Those accountants of his have been stuffing my head with figures, trying to bring me up to speed. I haven't had a moment to call my own.'

'Well, OK,' she said at last. 'That I can understand. But you never bother to keep in touch. I thought we were friends but you don't even send me text messages. You never spare me a thought from one week's end to another.'

'Now that isn't fair. I'm here now, aren't I? And I did bring you flowers.'

'Why do men always think that flowers will buy their way out of anything? My father is just the same. If he upsets Mim, he fills the whole house with flowers.'

'All right.' He shrugged dramatically. 'I agree with you. I'm a terrible person. What can I do to put it right?'

'Oh, come over here you—'

'And risk upsetting madame again? I don't think so.'

'Come over here and give me a kiss. Or you can forget about tomorrow, as well.'

He was there in an instant, still keeping a wary eye on Magenta. Fortunately, the filly had turned her attention to her hay bag. The kiss took a long time and was satisfying to both of them. He broke free eventually and looked into her eyes, his own soft and sleepy with lust. 'It's quite true,' he said, 'you're delicious—reeking of horses and salty girl sweat.'

'And you smell like a lounge lizard—all fresh linen and expensive cologne.'

'Lounge lizard? Where did that come from? I've never heard anyone use that expression but Grady.'

'And he picked it up from my pa who uses it to describe people who buy polo ponies to show off with rather than engage in serious sport. Put me down now, Jared, I'll mess up your suit.'

'I have others. Pa's old secretary, Olivia, made me buy a whole new wardrobe of them; the old bat wouldn't even let me choose my own ties.'

Alex smiled. 'Just the sort of person you need. I'd like to meet this Olivia.'

'No, you wouldn't. She's a dreadful harridan but I'm stuck with her because she knows Pa's business backwards. Been with the firm for over twenty years.'

'Poor you.' Alex tried to keep a straight face but couldn't help laughing. 'It must be like being back at school.'

'I assure you, it isn't funny. I used to think Pa was scared of her and now I'm beginning to know why.'

The following morning, Alex was up early to make sure Madge was properly groomed and would be seen to her best advantage at the track. Early on in the day, it was a fillies' race with just a small field and Magenta Magic would be at long odds if people remembered her disastrous outing in the city. Alex knew Grady was hoping for a good result from her this time and could only hope nothing would happen to unsettle her. Since she was the only entrant from the Allens' stables that day, she would travel alone in a single horse box with Mike and Alex.

Due to the wet weather at Cranbourne that day, Alex was relieved to see that few people, apart from owners and trainers, had taken the trouble to attend. Ordinary punters had chosen to watch their day's racing on television and in the comfort of their own homes.

Magenta strode around the mounting yard with her head high like a queen, looking so well that her odds shortened fifteen minutes before the race. Luckily, Mike had time to place a few dollars for both of them well before the start.

Tasha Trussardi mounted the horse with a confident smile and the crowd, although small, admired the big red filly as she galloped out on to the course and passed them on the way to the starting gates. She was certainly the largest horse in the field; it remained to be seen if she would be the fastest.

Sensing tension between them, Alex hesitated to join the Allen brothers in the stands. They didn't see her at first so, without intending to eavesdrop, she caught the last few sentences of their muttered but venomous exchange.

'I don't interfere in your business, Jared—'

'Hah! Chance would be a fine thing.'

'So I don't expect you to meddle in mine.'

'All the same, Bro, you should take his offer more seriously. It's a good chance to make money out of a horse that's been nothing but trouble since the day she arrived. Grab the chance to get rid of her before she does anything worse.'

'Jared, leave it,' Grady said through gritted teeth, aware that Alex was approaching and might even be close enough to hear what they were saying.

'All right. But never forget,' Jared said, determined to have the last word, 'the stables may be your concern but I hold the largest number of company shares and that gives me the controlling interest.'

'Forget it, Little Bro. It was never Pa's intention to let you get as much power as you have. So hands off my stables.'

Jared shrugged and turned to greet Alex, smiling widely as if he hadn't a care in the world. 'Hi there, Alex,' he greeted her breezily. 'How goes it?'

'Fine,' she said automatically, trying to make sense out of what she had just overheard.

'How did Magenta settle this time?' Grady said, ignoring his brother's small talk.

'Should go well.' Alex shrugged, telling him what he wanted to hear. ' 'Long as nothing happens to spook her.'

'Trussardi knows what she's doing. It's up to her now.' Grady raised his binoculars, watching the horses assembling behind the starting gates. 'Let's hope she can keep Madge out of trouble this time.'

Moments later, they were off. Madge bolted out of the stalls and took up the lead, setting a cracking pace. Seeing this, Grady winced, shaking his head.

'Look at that,' he groaned. 'Going too fast, too soon. She'll wear herself out and have nothing left when she gets to the straight.'

Alex watched the big red filly's progress but she didn't say anything. Madge liked to run her own race and Alex knew that if Tasha tried to slow her down now, the big filly would lose heart and give up.

It was only a short race and the home turn was upon them almost immediately. Taking advantage of her position to seize the most favourable ground in the straight, Madge lengthened her stride, increasing her lead. No one would catch her now. Tasha, riding high on her neck, didn't even need to show her the whip and Magenta Magic passed the winning post at least five lengths ahead of the rest of the field.

There was a concerted groan from the crowd and nobody cheered. She had been at long odds and most people had lost their money.

'See, Bro?' Jared nudged his brother. 'We should strike while the iron's hot.'

Ignoring him, Grady seized Alex and gave her a shoulder-crunching hug. 'Come on,' he said. 'Let's get down there and congratulate Tash.' Alex raced ahead of him, anxious to reclaim her horse. Madge could be unpredictable at the best of times and wasn't to be trusted, even after winning a race.

When Tasha had taken her saddle and gone to weigh in, a large middle-aged man in a suit accosted Grady while they were still standing in the winner's stall. He was smiling but he had cruel eyes, Alex thought; they were a cold, pale green. He had the opaque, dull grey skin of a life-long smoker and a habit of scratching the backs of his hands which were red and peeling from some skin disorder.

'Well, Grady'—he had one of those deep, gravelly voices so beloved by television advertisers—'have you thought any more of my offer? You won't get a better one and your brother's willing to close the deal. So whaddya say?'

'The answer's the same as before, Bill. Magenta isn't for sale.'

'For sale?' Alex gasped, staring at Grady. All her joy in winning had evaporated at the thought of losing Magenta. It was impossible, surely?

'Leave it, Alex. I'll deal with this.' Grady said. 'Take Madge back to the stables now and when you've tidied up and you're ready, you and Mike can take her home.'

'But—'

'Now, Alex.' He gave her a hard stare.

Suddenly wanting to put as much distance as she could between herself and those cold green eyes, Alex led the horse away, conscious all the time that the two men were watching them leave. Many questions seethed in her mind until she reminded herself of her date with Jared that evening; she would get to the bottom of the mystery then. She wouldn't spring it on him but would wait until they were seated at the dinner table where he would find it harder to avoid her queries and there would be no escape.

She showered and dressed carefully in a sexy, black silk cheongsam decorated with gold chrysanthemums. Having discovered it on her day off in her favourite vintage clothing shop, she had not yet had time to wear it. In order to match the sophistication of the dress, she had bought a new lip-gloss in a darker shade than she usually wore and now that her hair was growing again, she was able to pin it back with a matching artificial chrysanthemum tucked behind her ear. Her high-heeled gold sandals completed the picture. When she had finished dressing, Katrina sighed at her transformation with a mixture of admiration and envy.

'Oh, Alex,' she murmured. 'If only I could be tall like you. Sometimes, I feel so— inadequate.'

'But Katrina, you're lovely. Everyone says so.' Alex hugged her friend. 'Like a diminutive Gwyneth Paltrow.'

'With all these freckles?' Katrina laughed. 'I wish.'

'Gwyneth has freckles, too.' Alex reassured her and jumped with excitement as her mobile rang with a message. 'Have to go. Jared is waiting for me outside. See you later.'

'Yeah.' Katrina sighed again. 'I don't need to tell you to have a good time.'

'There'll be someone for you, I promise. I'm sure Jared has friends. We could make up a foursome. D'you want me to ask?'

'No!' Katrina looked horrified. 'Don't even mention it.'

But Alex was already running towards the door.

'Wow!' Jared said, when he caught sight of her. 'Is all this for me? You certainly know how to turn on the glamour, don't you?'

'You like?' Alex twirled to show him the dress.

'If the mood is Chinese tonight, we must go to a Chinese restaurant. I know just the place. Let's see if I can get us a table.'

As he did so with authority, overriding complaints that the restaurant was fully booked, Alex decided she could see many changes in Jared since his father's demise. Although he blamed Morris's old PA for his formal new wardrobe, his appearance was flawless and he was enjoying his new look. It might be an illusion but certainly he seemed more serious-minded, more mature. Even his car was new—a fire engine red Porsche Carrera. It even had red wheels.

'We can be in town in ten minutes if we take the new toll road.' He grinned. 'I look forward

146

to showing you what this little beauty can do.'

'Jared, I hate to be a spoilsport,' she said, biting her lip. 'But travelling at high speeds can make me feel sick.'

'Ooh no, not in this car,' he said. 'I'll drive like an old nanna, then. We can't have you losing your lunch before you've had dinner.'

'There's nothing to lose,' she said ruefully. 'I never had time for lunch.'

'Really?' He gave her an evil grin. 'So if I fill you up with cocktails—'

'Don't even think about it,' she said. 'Let's go.'

Jared was as good as his word and drove towards the city as sedately as if he were driving a vintage Daimler. At the same time Alex sensed his frustration at being overtaken by less powerful cars. She held her breath when some boys in a jazzed up old Falcon tried to tempt him into a drag race from a set of lights but after accelerating away from the junction to prove that he could leave them behind if he wanted to, Jared slowed down again, letting them race away with tyres screaming. They left trails of burning rubber on the road and leaned out of the car to scream insults as they went on their way. A mile or so up the road, Alex was amused to see that the car had been stopped behind an unmarked police car. The young hoons were standing beside it, looking crestfallen as the officers had their notebooks out and were examining every inch of the old Falcon to make sure it was roadworthy. Clearly, they wouldn't be resuming their journey any time soon.

The restaurant Jared favoured was attached to one of the top hotels in town. He left the Porsche to be valet parked and escorted Alex up the steps and through the revolving doors. The restaurant was on one of the higher floors and they were shown to a table with spectacular views of the river and the sprawl of the suburbs beyond. Ever since she was a child, Alex had visited restaurants with her father, but this one was almost intimidating in its formality. She watched Jared as he studied the menu, wondering if he would ask her what she wanted or if he would choose for both of them. An errant thought popped unbidden into her head. If she really were to become Jared's wife, meals such as this would be commonplace. And would she like it if they were? Wasn't it better to save such an outing for a special occasion? A treat?

'You're looking very serious.' Jared smiled, taking her hand.

'I was just wondering if I have to choose a meal or if you have something in mind?'

'Oh, you have to be guided by me. I know their best dishes—they don't do anything like the old sweet and sour with pineapple sauce. Not allergic to seafood are you?'

'No. I'm probably not so keen on pork—it

148

gives me a headache—but I can eat everything else.'

Jared ordered so much food that there was scarcely room on the table for their bowls and chopsticks. Alex tasted everything and said she enjoyed it all. She was secretly grateful that the cocktails hadn't materialized. In fact, they had nothing to drink at all apart from green tea.

'Right,' Jared said. 'Now we've demolished the main course, what would you like for dessert.'

'Nothing more,' she said, suppressing a ladylike burp. 'I couldn't eat another thing.'

'That's a shame,' he said. 'Because they make fritters to die for and their own ice cream.'

'You order one then and I'll taste yours.' She stood up. 'And while we're waiting for it, I'll just go to the powder room.'

In the powder room, she replaced her lip-gloss and adjusted the gold chrysanthemum in her hair, suddenly realizing that she had come to the attention of another girl. The girl staring at her was a teenager with long, blonde hair, pouting 'baby doll' looks and blue eyes although her gaze was anything but friendly. Alex decided it must be a case of mistaken identity; she had done nothing to provoke such bad feeling. She decided to get to the bottom of it by challenging the girl.

'Excuse me,' she said. 'But I saw you looking

at me. Do I know you?'

The girl didn't answer but blushed to the roots of her hair, snatched up her purse and flounced out of the room. Alex returned to their table to find her leaning over it, deep in conversation with Jared.

'Linda, I'm sorry,' he was saying, 'but I'm with a guest, as you see, and this really isn't the time.'

The girl stared at him as if she couldn't believe what she was hearing, tears swimming in her eyes. 'You can't treat me like this, Jared Allen,' she said in a tremulous voice. 'I'll make you pay—see if I don't.'

'Now, Linda.' He closed his eyes, trying to check his impatience. 'Hold it right there. I never said—never promised you anything.'

'No. You made sure of that, didn't you? You and your fatal charm.' She looked up, realizing that Alex had come back to the table and was watching the exchange with interest. 'Don't let him make a fool of you, too.' Blinded by tears, she ran from the room, almost colliding with a waiter carrying trays in her haste to get away.

Alex sat down opposite him, folding her arms. 'And that was?'

'Linda Carmichael. Or 'Babyface' as we used to call her. The little sister of one of my best friends.'

'Not all that little so far as I can see. And she seemed to think she had a closer acquaintance with you than that.'

'Oh, Alex, don't give me the third degree. We were having such a good time.' He paused, hoping she would let it go at that, but Alex studied him, with raised eyebrows, waiting for him to say more. 'All right—if you must know, then I'll tell you. Linda has had this crush on me since she was twelve and, like a fool, I used to tease her about it. We all expected her to grow out of it, but she hasn't.'

'Hmm. And what did this "teasing" involve?'

'Oh God, I don't know. Nothing. Alex, the kid is barely sixteen. Can we talk about something else, please?'

'Yeah. Because there's something I've been meaning to ask you all evening. What was that scrap you had with Grady at the races?'

'It was nothing.' He tried to smile, but his face was settling into sullen lines. 'What is this? If you're determined to spoil a lovely evening, I'd better take you home.'

'Jared, you can't expect me to take you seriously if you lie by omission and hide things from me all the time. Well, I can put two and two together—'

'And make five!'

'You want Grady to sell Magenta, don't you? To that horrible man with the cruel eyes.'

'Bill Baranski's not cruel, he's just unsentimental. A professional, that's all. He's looking for promising young horses to take back to Adelaide.'

151

'Not Madge! She might have looked good today but you know she needs special care.'

'You could buy two Madges for what Baranski was willing to offer. Hell, Alex. That brute is nothing but trouble. She put you in hospital.' He turned over her arm to examine the angry red marks on her wrist. 'See? You still bear the scars.'

'That wasn't her fault.' She glared at him, snatching her arm away. 'And anyway, I don't care.'

'You're getting yourself in a state over nothing. Grady won't sell.'

'Are you sure?'

'Unless Baranski comes up with an offer he can't refuse.' Jared shrugged, applying himself to his dessert until he looked up and saw that Alex's eyes were awash with tears. 'Only kidding. I'm sorry, Alex. I know I shouldn't make jokes about something that matters so much to you.'

'I'm sorry, too.' Alex took a deep breath and swallowed her tears. 'I never meant to cause trouble and spoil our evening.'

'Let's start over, shall we?' Jared took her hand and kissed the tips of her fingers, making her shiver. 'Have I told you, Miss Hay, that you are looking especially lovely tonight?'

CHAPTER EIGHT

At that point Alex knew that the evening could only end one of two ways. She would have to burn her bridges and spend the rest of the night with him or send him on his way. As yet, she hadn't made her mind up which it was to be. She wasn't an innocent, far from it, although her father wouldn't be pleased to hear it and, in hindsight, she wasn't proud of what she had done. In an act of bravado, she had given or rather thrown away her virginity when she was at boarding-school.

Without too much thought for the raging hormones of boys and girls in their mid teens, the head teacher had arranged a combined social event with a neighbouring boys' school. Under the supposedly watchful eyes of their teachers, the party took place in their school hall with doors opening on to steps leading down to the tree-lined grounds. Temptation beckoned and she wasn't the only one to slip away and take advantage of such an opportunity.

The young man in question had been dark haired, good-looking and all her friends fancied him. But he had eyes for no one but Alex who already stood a head taller than most other girls. Dared by her friends and a victim of curiosity rather than passion, she had let him make love to her against the trunk of one of the trees. It wasn't a happy experience; furtive, uncomfortable and messy, leaving her disappointed and ashamed of her part in this loveless act. Later, she felt guilty and sad about her lack of feelings for the boy who kept trying to contact her, unable to understand why she didn't want to see him again.

Staring at Jared's profile now as they drove home, she considered her options. She already knew that she wanted him. But her previous experience was making her cautious. What if his love-making didn't match up to her expectations? Would she cast him off as heartlessly as she had dumped that other boy? And what if it were the other way around? Was Jared one of those men who lived mainly for the chase? Having caught her, would he toss her aside like Linda Carmichael? She had a gut feeling there was a lot more to that story than he was telling.

Of course, the sensible thing to do would be to go home, get out of the car and say *Thank you, Jared, and good night* but Alex had never been one to take easy options. So, when he drove from the highway, taking a steep incline towards the beach, she didn't protest. And, when he finally stopped the car in a car-park on top of a cliff, deserted apart from the whispering of the waves on the shore far below, the silence was almost deafening. They had driven from the city both lost in thought and with very few words passing between them. He hadn't suggested music and, without the soothing purr of the engine, the tension between them was almost palpable as Jared leaned over to assess Alex's mood as he looked into her eyes. She held his gaze for a moment and then looked down at her hands in her lap, waiting for him to make the next move.

'What is it Alex?' he said at last. 'Is anything wrong? You're very quiet.'

She sighed. 'I suppose I have a lot to think about tonight. To decide.'

'Such as?'

She took a deep breath and told him the truth. 'I don't know if I should sleep with you or not.'

'Ah,' he said, sitting back in his seat. She was half hoping he would make the decision for her, seizing her in his arms and kissing her doubts away but he didn't.

'We don't have to do this now, Alex, if it's not what you want,' he said at last. 'I know how girls feel about the first time and realize you must be—'

'It isn't the first time and I'm not a virgin.' She blurted the words, not at all certain how he would react.

'Well,' he said, clearly surprised but trying to make light of it. 'Who is—these days?'

'I didn't enjoy it, though, so it might not count.'

155

He burst out laughing then, making her frown. 'Oh, Alex, that is so—only you could think that.'

'Must you make a joke out of everything?' She was close to tears now. 'Perhaps you should take me home after all.'

He took a deep breath, suppressing his laughter. 'I'm sorry but I don't take the loss of virginity all that seriously, my love. We're not living in the dark ages. And how can I blame you for something that happened before we met? Especially as you tell me you didn't enjoy it. Any more than I'd expect you to blame me for having a past.'

'I'm sure your past is a lot more colourful than mine.'

'Let's not go there, shall we? I've come here to kiss you, not argue with you.' He took the flower out of her hair and took his time about kissing her ear. No one had done that to Alex before and she found it incredibly sensual. He kissed her throat, gently at first and then viciously, almost like a vampire's bite, making her gasp. She knew there would be a bruise to explain in the morning. She felt warm all over, longing for him to touch her body but his kisses, although passionate, were also teasing, making her wait. Her breathing quickened and her throat felt dry.

'Oh, Jared,' she groaned. 'Can't you—?'

'Unfortunately, there's no back seat,' he murmured. 'But I'm sure the passenger seat can accommodate us, if we're careful.' His lips twitched in a mischievous smile. 'Unless you'd rather come back to my place?'

'There isn't time! I can't think of anything except that I need you—right now.'

'OK, then. I'm game, if you are. Let's christen my new car.'

While she unfastened the cheongsam and left it in the space behind the seats where it wouldn't get crushed he came round to her side of the car. He opened the door and laid her seat back as far as it would go—a little too expertly, she thought, making her wonder if he really hadn't done this before. She crossed her arms across her breasts, shivering from anticipation as well as the sudden chill from the open door. He took off his jacket and tore off his shirt and tie, flinging them on to the driver's seat, before easing himself into the seat beside her and closing the door.

'I'll make you warm again soon,' he whispered. Sensing her sudden reluctance he kissed her deeply to bring back the mood. Sighing, she let herself relax into it, enjoying the sensation of his muscular body pressed close against her own.

Almost without realizing it, he removed her black lace bikini panties, leaving her unashamedly naked.

'Oh, Alex, you're even more beautiful than I thought.' He took her breasts in his hands, teasing her nipples with sensitive fingers and

157

making her moan with pleasure. 'All this loveliness just for me.' He unfastened his trousers and had her feel his readiness, hot and heavy in her hands. Although Alex professed to know what she was doing, this was a new experience entirely, nothing like what had happened before. That boy at school had scarcely penetrated her and then come in her knickers, disgusting her. Jared's lovemaking was both leisurely and considerate as he watched her progress through the various stages, bringing her to a peak of longing. At last, when she could bear it no longer, he put on a condom and pulled her towards him, lifting her on to him, making her cry out in both pleasure and pain.

'Wait a moment!' she said. 'Oh, Jared, I'm still not sure—'

'Too late, my darling. I am,' he muttered, far beyond any thought of withdrawal now. For just a moment she could have sworn a look of triumph passed over his face to be gone in a second, making her wonder if she had seen it at all. 'Just stay with me, sweets, and the pleasure will be all yours.'

He was right. As a young, healthy example of womanhood, Alex experienced her first orgasm and was very soon hungry for more. The windows of the car steamed with condensation as the couple lay there, intent on exploring each other and totally oblivious to the passing of several hours.

'Oh, Jared, where did the time go?' She wailed as she scrabbled on the floor for her panties some hours later and tried to struggle into her dress. This was impossible and she had to get out of the car and stand up in order to do so. 'The last time I looked at my watch it was nearly midnight and now it's almost three. I have to be with Magenta in under an hour!'

'No, you don't.' Jared looked irritated at the mention of the filly. 'Katrina's your friend, isn't she? Get her to start the morning chores and say you'll be there when you can. Have a kip on the way in the car, then run in and change. No one will be any the wiser.'

He didn't mean any of this. Instead of moving in quietly, allowing Alex to escape without creating a fuss, Jared drove the Porsche up the drive like a racing car, creating a bow wave of gravel until they came to a screeching halt outside the dormitories. The stables were already a blaze of lights with people working there.

'You did that on purpose.' Alex accused him.

'So? Why should we sneak about?' Jared was suddenly hard. 'I want everyone to know you're my girl and that we're about to be married.'

Before she could protest and say it was still early days, Toby and Mike came out of the stables, followed by Grady who came up to the car, hands on hips. Hardly able to meet his gaze, Alex knew exactly what he must be seeing—a girl with wild hair, flushed cheeks, bruised lips and, most damning of all, an angry bruise on her throat in the shape of Jared's teeth.

'And before you say anything, Bro.' Jared made certain to get in first. 'Alexis is no longer your stable girl slave. We really are going to be married. Soon.'

Grady subjected Alex to another top to toe inspection and when he finally spoke, it seemed as if the words stuck in his throat and it pained him to speak. His expression remained closed, unreadable. 'Congratulations, Jared. Somehow you always get what you want.' He was speaking so softly that Alex could scarcely hear him. 'I hope you'll both be very happy.'

Alex climbed out of the car and walked towards the girls' dormitory like an old woman; she didn't even have the heart to say 'goodnight' to Jared who turned his car and roared off down the driveway, not caring if he disturbed the horses and leaving another bow wave of stones in his wake.

'I'll be there in five,' she spoke to Grady over her shoulder. 'Soon as I've changed.'

'Don't bother, Alex,' he said, making her flinch at his tone. 'Katrina has already seen to everything. Just go to bed and get some rest. You look as if you need it.'

Inside, Alex looked at herself in the mirror

160

and saw that her worst fears had been realized. She looked like a tramp. Her hair was tousled, her dress remained unfastened at the neck, she had more than one bruise on her throat and her lips were swollen and raw, making her look if she'd taken part in an all night orgy.

She undressed, showered, put on a clean nightgown and got into bed although she was far too tense to get any sleep. Running over the evening's events in her mind, she reached several conclusions. Certainly, she had enjoyed making love with Jared, but wasn't he pushing everything forward much too fast? And why did he want to marry her with such urgency when their relationship had scarcely begun? There was plenty of time, after all— they were both so young. Then she paused, remembering something else. Something that wasn't quite right. He had never actually *asked* her to marry him—he had always assumed it.

She also considered their different lifestyles. Jared's new home and business interests were in town while her place was here with Magenta. He'd never asked if she was willing to give that up. And what was that he said to his brother? 'Alexis is no longer your stable girl slave—we're going to be married,' almost taunting him with this news. She didn't think of herself as a slave here at all but if she were to marry Jared she might well end up as a housewife/slave in his fancy apartment.

But she was also a creature of passion and when she thought of his love making and how he had roused her, she suppressed all these doubts, hungry for him all over again. Hadn't she fallen in love from the very first moment she saw him? She was a fool to lie here splitting hairs, thinking Jared unromantic, even calculating in his pursuit of her. Of course he loved her—didn't actions speak louder than words? To be sure, there was still a lot to discuss. After all her hard work with Magenta, could she really turn her back on the horse, just as she was about to realize her full potential? But other people were involved now—Grady and Tasha Trussardi, not forgetting Katrina who had covered for her more than once. But she couldn't forget the bond she had forged with this particular horse. Was she really content to get married and walk away, leaving this part of her life behind?

And then there was Grady. He didn't seem happy about it at all, offering his congratulations as if the words choked him. Why? Did he disapprove of her even though Dad was his friend? It was all very puzzling and didn't really make sense. At last, unable to reach a satisfactory conclusion to anything, Alex fell into an uneasy sleep.

*   *   *

After this, things started happening very quickly, as if Jared was in a hurry to cement the relationship, leaving her no time to think. He took her on a special package tour of Melbourne, beginning with an afternoon helicopter ride over the city, where the pilot pointed out all the main landmarks of Melbourne—there was the Melbourne Cricket Ground, the Shrine of Remembrance, Government House, the Yarra winding its way sluggishly towards the sea, as well as the tall, glass palaces of the city, stretching upwards as if they were trying to touch the sky.

'This is *my* city,' Jared told her. 'And I need you to love it as I do. It will be your city, too, once we are married.'

'Yes, Jared,' she said. 'I need to talk to you about that—' But she broke off, realizing he wasn't listening, giving his attention to what the pilot was saying instead.

And when they touched down, there was a limo waiting to take them on the next stage of their journey. Entering one of the towering buildings in the heart of Melbourne, they entered the lift only to experience the sensation of visibility on all sides as they hurtled upwards. Alex closed her eyes, biting her lip and hoping not to be overtaken by vertigo while Jared laughed, almost enjoying her discomfiture.

'Where are we going?' She whispered to him when they arrived. 'Is it a restaurant?'

'Not really,' he said. 'But we'll have supper here. They call it "the highest dining experience in the Southern hemisphere".'

When they arrived, Jared allowed her to sit back and relish her surroundings. It was a clear, cool night and the sprawl of the city was visible for some miles. So enchanted was Alex with the view, that she scarcely took note of what she was eating, until at last the chocolate mousse arrived, along with coffee.

Jared smiled at her guilt-free enjoyment of the delicious sweet and pushed a small, black velvet box towards her across the table.

'I do realize,' he said, 'that I haven't done things in the right order. I've been so anxious to marry you that I haven't even asked you properly, have I?'

'Well, I'm so pleased you raised it, Jared, because I need to talk to you about that.'

Once more ignoring what she had to say, Jared sprung open the box to reveal the largest diamond Alex had ever set eyes on except in the window of a jeweller's store.

'Marry me, Alex. Just say "yes" so I can put it on.'

'Jared, it's gorgeous of course. But I can't accept something like that. I work with horses, remember? My hands wouldn't do it justice. And when would I ever be able to wear it?'

'All the time when you're with me.'

'But our lives are so impossibly different.'

'Different, yes. Impossibly, no.' He slipped

164

the ring on her finger. 'See? It fits. Just like Cinderella's slipper. That's a good omen.'

'Oh, Jared.'

'Stop looking so worried. You do love me, don't you? All you have to do is relax and let everything fall into place.'

'But there's still Magenta—we haven't talked about—'

'Stop stressing about that wretched filly. I'm beginning to think she's cast a spell on you as well as my brother.'

'It's not that. I just think we should slow down a little. I don't see how I can be your wife and live in your town house as well as pursue my own dream of helping to make a great racehorse out of Magenta.'

'Exactly. Helping. You are neither the trainer nor the jockey, remember?'

'Don't belittle my role.'

'Sorry, sorry.' Jared cringed, realizing he'd made a wrong move. 'But I feel you're creating obstacles where there are none. You don't have to live in town.'

'Why not? I don't understand.' She squinted at the ring, finding it large and incongruous on her slender hand.

He shrugged. 'I'm busy from Monday to Friday and sometimes I have to go interstate for days at a time. If you were living in town, you wouldn't see much of me, anyway. You'd be on your own.'

'Isn't that another reason why we should

165

wait?'

'Not at all. You can stay at the country house all week and do what you have to do with the horses. I could join you at weekends.'

She stared at him. 'But what about Grady?'

'What about him?' Jared shrugged.

'Well, it's *his* house, isn't it? As he made very clear at your father's funeral. I can't live there alone with your brother—it wouldn't be right.'

Jared smiled wickedly. 'I'm sure my brother's enough of a gentleman not to take unfair advantage. In any case, you wouldn't be living alone with him—the housekeeper's there.'

She shook her head, unconvinced. 'Jared, this isn't going to work. It sounds very much like a part-time marriage to me.'

'It's all down to you, sweets. Come live with me and give up Magenta, or settle for the part-time option. To start with, at least. The choice is yours.'

She started to slide the ring off her finger. 'I'm not even sure I'm ready to make it. There's just too much to think about—to decide. As I said before, I think we should slow down a little and wait.'

Jared reached across and pushed it back on. 'No. I won't lose you.' He hesitated, little boy lost again. 'Unless you really don't love me, after all?'

'Oh Jared, you know I do.' She whispered,

raising her eyes to stare into his smouldering blue gaze. Her heart lurched, confirming it as she did so.

'Then, we won't hesitate. You're going to be Mrs Jared Allen before the year is out.'

'It wouldn't be right. We can't have a wedding so soon after burying your father.'

'Don't be so old-fashioned. Whatever we do can't hurt him now. And Mother's safely out of the way in Queensland. Talking of going on a cruise now—on the lookout for her next husband, no doubt.'

'You really don't approve of her lifestyle, do you?'

Jared shrugged. 'She's a hypocrite. There's always been one rule for her and another for me.'

If that's what he thought of his mother, it occurred to Alex that there were very few people Jared trusted or liked—with the possible exception of his father's old secretary, Olivia.

He caught her hand, quickly kissing the tips of her fingers. 'With the wedding out of the way, I can concentrate on building my business. Pa left a good basic structure but there's always room for improvement. Now, let's have a glass of champagne to celebrate.'

Once again he parked the car and made love to her on the way home. With perhaps even greater intensity than he had shown before. But this time he brought her home quietly without making a show of it and, as she climbed the stairs to the dormitory she shared with Katrina, she studied the unfamiliar diamond, winking like a torch lighting her way.

She tiptoed around, undressing in the dark, until her friend spoke up in the darkness, her voice still heavy with sleep.

'S'all right, Alex, I'm awake. You can switch on the bedside light.'

Alex did so and sat on the side of Katrina's bed, her attention caught once again by the weight of that unfamiliar ring on her finger. Katrina followed the direction of her gaze.

'My God, what's that? It's blinding. Did you steal Elizabeth Taylor's diamond?'

'No.' Alex had to smile although her voice was only a whisper. 'But I don't blame you for thinking so. That's my engagement ring.'

'From Jared?'

'Uhuh.' Alex sighed, offering her hand for Katrina's inspection.

'Wow. Aren't you scared of losing it?'

'Yes. But Jared insisted.'

'So what's the matter now?' Katrina narrowed her eyes. 'For someone newly engaged, you seem a trifle glum. Why aren't you over the moon?'

Alex shrugged. 'Maybe I don't realize it as yet. Or it hasn't sunk in.'

'And when it does?' Katrina quizzed her, head on one side. 'Is this engagement likely to

168

be a long one?'

'I'd prefer it that way but Jared wants to be married in just a few weeks.'

Katrina blew out her cheeks. 'A whirlwind romance then.'

'It's just that everything feels so rushed.'

'Lots of girls would be thrilled to be swept off their feet in that way—me included.'

'Yeah but I'm worried about what will happen when we come down to earth.'

'Oh, I know all about that. Boring dinner parties for his business associates.' Katrina laughed as Alex pulled a face. 'Then you'll be expected to found a dynasty. Before you know it, you'll be in the midst of kids and diapers.'

'Ugh! You're making me feel as if I don't want to be married at all.'

'Then speak up and say so—if you'd rather not.'

'I've asked Jared to wait but he won't listen.' Alex twisted the ring on her finger. 'He made it pretty clear that I have to do this now or I'll lose him.'

'That's emotional blackmail.' Kat looked severe. 'And you really haven't known him that long. You shouldn't let yourself be railroaded into something you might regret.'

'Easy for you to say. You're not the one riding this roller-coaster of emotions. Of course I'm in love with Jared—'

'Or in lust.'

'Stop it. And of course I want to marry him.

169

Wouldn't anyone? But I wasn't expecting to tie the knot just yet.'

'You still don't sound like a fully committed bride to me.'

'All right, I'll show you how committed I can be. You'll be my bridesmaid, Kat, won't you?'

'Certainly not!' Katrina snapped back without a moment's thought, making Alex lift her head and stare at her in surprise. 'I can't abide weddings, funerals—or any of those archaic human rituals.'

'Why?'

'Does it matter?'

'No. But if you won't do it, I'll have to make do with my ditzy cousin Jen.'

'You do that, Alex. Ditzy or not, she'll be a lot more use to you than I'd ever be.'

CHAPTER NINE

Wedding preparations didn't mean that Alex neglected Madge. If anything, she became more devoted to the difficult filly than ever before. And, if her father was surprised by this sudden decision to marry, he kept most of his opinions to himself. By now he was all too aware of his daughter's wilfulness and realized that opposition on his part only fanned the flames.

The wedding was set to take place on a

Friday morning at the end of September. Unwilling to give Madge up to the care of Katrina or any other strapper for the duration of the Spring Carnival, Alex had chosen to fall in with Jared's plan to move into Grady's house after the wedding. Jared himself would give full attention to his business affairs during the week and join her at the old homestead over the weekend.

They both knew this wasn't an ideal state of affairs for newly-weds but, if Jared wanted the wedding out of the way to pursue his business interests, she was just as eager to return to her normal routine with Madge, especially during the preparation for the filly's first Carnival when she would need special care. Alex had already moved the bulk of her clothing—which wasn't a great deal—into the walk-in wardrobe of the spacious room she was to share with Jared.

The only person who seemed thrilled with the prospect of her step daughter's marriage was Mim, visibly pregnant now and looking forward to motherhood. Three days before the wedding, she welcomed Alex back to her old home with more enthusiasm than she had ever displayed before. All the same, she lost no time in mentioning that, once Alex was gone for good, she would turn her old bedroom into a nursery for the expected baby.

'I shall paint everything a nice sunny yellow,' she said, patting the burgeoning roundness of her belly. 'Then it won't matter if it's a boy or a girl.'

And she smiled like a conspirator as she helped Alex to unpack her wedding gown and shake out the creases before hanging it on the back of the bedroom door.

'I didn't know you had it in you, Alex,' she said. 'How clever of you to snare Jared Allen. I'd say he has every prospect of ending up even wealthier than his father.'

'I'm not marrying him for his money, if that's what you think.'

'Of course not, my dear, there's no need to be sensitive. I'm just pointing out that you're a very fortunate girl.'

*　　　*　　　*

Although the timing was bad, Vere had to be at the airport, supervising the arrival of two polo ponies from overseas and arranging their quarantine, leaving Alex and his wife alone.

'Try not to kill one another while I'm away,' he said, meaning it as a joke but it fell flat as the two women looked at each other and didn't smile.

'Don't tempt me.' Alex muttered under her breath.

Fortunately, that same day her cousin Jennifer arrived to stay until after the wedding and Jared promised to take them both out to lunch. Much the same age as Alex, Jennifer

172

was a plump blonde with natural corkscrew curls and possessed of an infectious giggle. As they sat at lunch, Alex looked from one to the other watching them assess each other and hoping they were going to get along.

'So tell me, Jared, who's going to be your best man?' Jen said, giggling more than usual and pink in the face after two glasses of champagne. 'Somebody scrumptious, I hope?'

'Not really. Just my older brother, Grady.' Jared pulled a wry face. 'Sorry to disappoint. It was to have been my best friend, Buzz Carmichael, but he's something hush-hush in the military and got posted overseas.'

'Oh, what a shame. I do so love a man in uniform.' Jen gave a delicious shiver.

'So rather than do without a best man, Grady has to fill in.'

Jen wriggled her shoulders and pouted. 'And what makes you think I won't like this brother of yours? Married, I suppose. All the good ones are.'

'Single and likely to remain so.' Jared shrugged. 'Cares about nothing but horses. He's a lot older than I am—nine years to be exact. And serious minded to a fault. I don't think he knows how to have any fun.'

'Now that isn't fair—' Alex said, unwilling to listen to Jared tearing his brother down, but Jennifer broke in before she could say anything in his defence.

'All right, Jared. You owe me. Soon as your

friend—Buzz, wasn't it?—gets home from his tour of duty, I want an intro. If possible the day he gets back before he has time to meet anyone else. Shake on it.' She held out her hand to seal the bargain. Alex groaned, half expecting her cousin to spit on it first.

Jared shook it and then surprised the girl by turning her hand and kissing the palm. Jen withdrew it with a little shriek, fluttering her eyelashes and assuming a pose like the heroine of an old-fashioned drama. 'Fie, sir. Playing fast and loose with my affections. And you to be married the day after tomorrow.'

Everyone laughed it off but later, when Jared had made his excuses and left, Jen couldn't help telling Alex how lucky she was.

*   *   *

The next day Alex woke up really early around the time she would normally go to Magenta to attend to her morning needs. Missing her more than she expected, she decided to sneak away and pay a surprise visit to the stables. Before leaving for a whole week's honeymoon to a destination so secret that only Jared knew of it, she wanted to reassure herself that Madge was going to be OK.

It was still dark when she pulled up alongside the homestead although lights were appearing in the dormitories as everyone started to get up, forcing themselves awake under hot showers and preparing to greet a new day. Katrina wasn't in the room they once shared and Alex concluded that she must be hard at work in the stables.

She went down to Madge's stall at the end of the block, expecting to find Katrina there, preparing the filly for her morning's work. She had been designated to look after her while Alex was away. Instead, Alex was surprised to find the horse standing alone and neglected with no evidence that anyone had been near her so far. Madge whinnied, nuzzling her and nipping her pockets in the hope of a treat.

'Poor girl,' Alex murmured, seeing that no fresh hay had been added to her bag and what remained of her drinking water was dirty. 'This isn't good enough. I'll have something to say to Kat when I see her.' At the same time, she reminded herself, that not all strappers had been brought up on Belvedere Hay's exacting standards.

As she set to, tidying the stall and sweeping the night's manure into a corner, ready to collect, she became aware of unusual sounds from the stall next door; a stall she knew had been left empty for some time. She could hear muffled grunting and gasping, followed by a low moan as if somebody might be in pain.

Becoming scared that someone was being attacked and not knowing what she might find, Alex picked up a shovel, approached

175

with caution and, soundlessly, opened the door a few inches so that she could look in and see who was in there without being seen. As her eyes became accustomed to the gloom, she pushed it open a little further to see more.

Jared, the man she was due to marry the very next day, was having rough sex with a girl. What he was doing to her was too basic and crude to be called 'making love' as he forced her back against the outside wall of the stable, making her groan with every thrust. In too much of a hurry to undress, they were both fully clothed except that their pants were down around their knees. Jared was supporting himself with both hands on the wall as he drove into her as if his life depended on it, pushing the girl back against the bricks with every stroke. Lost to his own pleasure, he neither realized nor cared that she might not be enjoying herself as much as he was. Her face was pale and drawn and her eyes tightly closed but some sixth sense must have warned her that someone was watching them. She opened her eyes to look directly at Alex standing there and the ghost of a smile played briefly around her lips.

Sickened, Alex allowed the door to close silently, hiding them from view. She set down the shovel and moved away, unable to watch any more. Her legs were shaking as if they could scarcely support her. The fact that Jared had betrayed her on the eve of their wedding

176

was bad enough—and he could have chosen any one of the girls who worked in the stables—she knew how they envied her. But his partner in this frantic coupling was Katrina. The one person she had considered a friend. How could Kat betray her in this way—and in the stables of all places, where, in less than half an hour, strappers and riders would be arriving to go about their daily tasks. It seemed as if they wanted to advertise their affair, half hoping to be found out.

Her instinct now was to get away quickly before anyone saw her. She couldn't bear to meet up with Grady, Toby, or even Mike, knowing it would be impossible to pretend that nothing was wrong. As she was running towards her car, Grady came out of the house and waved a hand in greeting, signalling that he wanted to talk.

Unable to trust herself to say anything without breaking down, she smiled widely and tapped her watch, indicating that she didn't have time. She gave what she hoped was a cheery wave, flung the car in gear and quickly drove away. She could only hope he wouldn't mention to Jared that he had seen her—it would be hard to explain why she had come all this way without talking to him.

And Katrina! No wonder she didn't want to be her bridesmaid. Dozens of questions sprang to mind. Was this the first time? Or was it an affair of long standing; something that had happened many times before?

She drove towards Wonga Park automatically, not realizing how hard she was crying until she was blinded by tears and forced to pull off the road. She found some tissues in the glove box and wept in earnest, burying her head in her hands until she had cried it out. Then she blew her nose, repaired as much damage as she could and set off once more for her father's home.

So what was she to do now? Several courses lay open to her. The easiest would be to ignore what she'd seen and go through with the wedding as planned. She might even fool herself into thinking it hadn't happened. Or she could be brave and call it off, causing an almighty fuss and having to leave the stables, losing her job with Madge. Would Jared really care all that much if she did? Looking back over the months of their whirlwind relationship, she could see he had never behaved like a man who was deeply in love.

Not for the first time, she asked herself why, why on earth he had been so keen to marry her? They were both so young and it was obvious now that he was far from ready to make a commitment and settle down. For that matter, was she? And all those visits he made to Sydney and Brisbane. Were they really 'on business'? Or just an alibi for him to spend time with other girls? Was she ready to accept a part-time marriage? A husband who would be away all week, never saying where he was or who he was with?

Or had she read the situation all wrong? Instead of the conventional bucks' night with a strippogram, was that encounter with Katrina, Jared's version of a final fling? After all, they hadn't yet exchanged any vows and, so far as the law was concerned, he was still free to do as he pleased. But if he really loved her, why should he want a liaison with Katrina or any other girl? The more she thought about it, the less clearly she could see what to do.

Fortunately, when she got back to her father's house, she found no one at home. Mim left a note that she had gone shopping and that Alex should call if there was anything she needed. *What about a new bridegroom?* she thought, smiling ruefully.

There was also a note from Jen saying that she was meeting some friends at a café in town and inviting Alex to join them. She sent Jen a text message, crying off. The last thing she needed was Jen and her girl friends telling her how lucky she was.

*   *   *

In the end, she did nothing. By the time Mim and Jen returned, bringing tales of the people they'd seen and the bargains they found, she was almost herself again and, if they thought she was unusually quiet, they put it down to

179

pre-wedding jitters. Vere came home just before dinner, full of praise for his new horses but frustrated with the endless forms he had to fill in before they could be released to quarantine.

'I'm so sick of driving to the airport.' He caught Alex's hand and kissed it. 'It will be nice to do something different tomorrow. I'm looking forward to being father of the bride.'

'Dad, we need to talk—' Alex said.

But as usual Mim interrupted, cutting across what her stepdaughter had to say. 'You can thank me for collecting your suit from the cleaners, Vere. Good thing I didn't trust you to remember.'

'Thanks, my love.' Vere smiled at her, looking tired. 'You know I never think about clothes.'

'Just as well somebody does,' Mim put in, acid as ever.

Soon after that, she suggested everyone had an early night and the moment was gone.

Alex didn't get a good night's rest. Unable to sleep at first, she tossed and turned until the early hours. And when she finally fell into an exhausted slumber, she was plagued by dreams of Katrina dressed up in her wedding gown, prancing triumphantly towards the wedding party while Alex herself stood shivering, half naked in her underclothes.

She awoke to the sound of Jen knocking on her bedroom door.

'Today's the big day, Alex! Wake up, sleepyhead.'

Alex groaned, wanting to go back under the covers and retreat from the world until it was all too late. But she knew that wasn't an option. So she allowed Jen to haul her out of bed and push her under the shower, complaining all the time about her lack of enthusiasm.

'Wedding day, indeed,' Jen grumbled. 'Didn't know you were the nervous sort. Anyone would think you were going to your doom.'

Alex shrugged.

'Well, you're lucky that I'm a beautician.' She subjected Alex to a critical gaze when she emerged from the shower, still wan and red-eyed from lack of sleep. 'I'll need my whole box of tricks to make a glamour girl out of you.'

Alex said nothing, giving herself up to Jen's none-too-gentle attentions. She winced as her hair was pulled severely back from her face and secured with a false chignon.

'Why you had to cut off your beautiful hair, I'll never know,' Jen continued to moan. 'It'll take years to get any length back into it.'

Alex shrugged again, having nothing to offer. She was still hoping some outside influence would show her what to do.

'We are morose today, aren't we?' Jen kept talking to herself. 'Never mind. Just hold still

181

while I try to do something about that miserable face.'

Half an hour later, the bride's face had been made up to Jen's satisfaction. Alex stared at herself in the mirror, scarcely recognizing this glamorous creature as herself and just as uncertain whether to go through with the ceremony or not.

'Sit still and don't mess with anything till I get back,' Jen ordered. 'I'll get dressed myself and then I'll come and help you.'

Finally, the moment had come when she couldn't delay any more. Mim had been scolding everyone, ruining any moments of tenderness that might have taken place between Alex and her father. But at last Vere sensed his daughter's misgivings and suggested that, even at this late hour, she should cancel the wedding if she had any doubts.

But Alex didn't want to have any doubts. She wanted to return to that cocoon of happy ignorance in which she'd been living before. So she smiled bravely and kept insisting that everything would be OK.

It was only when she reached the scene where the marriage was to take place that all her uncertainties came flooding back. She had kept Jared waiting for almost an hour and the wedding guests were now restive as well, fidgeting on their uncomfortable chairs. The marriage celebrant was frowning and examining his watch—probably already late for somebody else's wedding. Grady stole a glance at her and she tried to smile at him but he looked away, his expression strained. But nothing could have prepared her for Jared's hostility. He was glowering at her, scarcely able to conceal his rage as he watched her approach through narrowed eyes. She was certain that sooner or later he would punish her for making him wait so long.

And then, as if someone had switched on a light in her mind, Alex knew what she had to do. Even as she walked towards him on her father's arm with Jen attending the veil a few paces behind her, she knew it would be a dreadful mistake to marry this spoilt, greedy man who would take her for granted and make her life a misery.

As soon as Alex arrived before him, the marriage celebrant started his spiel, almost gabbling in his anxiety not to waste any more time. It was hard for her to interrupt the practised flow of his speech and she had to raise her voice more than once to make him do so.

'I'm s-sorry—but I can't do this.' At last she had his attention. 'You have to stop.'

She threw her bouquet at Jennifer who was staring at her, open-mouthed, as she tore off the hampering veil and flung it aside. She kicked off her high-heeled pumps and, before the astonished gaze of family and friends, she hitched up her skirts and ran from that scene as fast as her long legs could carry her. She could hear shocked exclamations and the buzz of excited conversation behind her but, without really thinking where she was going, instinctively she headed for the stables.

As always, when she was upset, she wanted the silent comfort and empathy she always received from a horse. She paused in the doorway of Madge's stall, having quite forgotten that Katrina would be there. Katrina was equally startled and widened her eyes at the unusual sight of Alex, standing barefooted in the doorway, her wedding dress dragging on the ground. She suppressed a nervous giggle.

'Alex?' She said. 'What are you doing here? Aren't you supposed to be getting married today?'

'Get out of here, Katrina.' She was so angry with her one-time friend, she could scarcely speak. 'You've taken enough from me, already. I don't want you around my horse.'

'Ohh, la di da! I haven't taken anything Jared wasn't willing to give. Seems you weren't quite enough woman for him, were you?'

'Out!' Alex yelled, for once not caring that she was upsetting Madge.

By this time Jared had joined them, red in the face with fury. Katrina took one look at his expression and fled although Alex had the impression that she was smothering nervous

184

laughter. Before Alex had time to avoid it, he gave her a back-handed slap in the face, the force of which almost felled her, splitting her lip with one of his rings. Madge squealed and reared, meaning to trample him but he was too quick for her. Roughly, he grabbed Alex by the arm and pulled her out of the stall before flinging her hard against the opposite wall. Her head snapped back against it and her knees gave way as she slid down towards the floor, momentarily stunned.

'Bitch!' he yelled at her. 'I won't let anybody make me look a fool.'

Alex's head was spinning with dizziness and she tasted blood. She was now aware that, if nothing else, she had saved herself from marrying a wife-beater. Jared was out of control and she closed her eyes, bracing herself for what was to come, certain she was to receive the beating of her life. As he moved in again, lifting her by the upper arms as he decided where to strike next, she smelled the alcohol on his breath. He had been drinking even before the wedding feast.

But just as suddenly he was out of her face and she could see daylight again. Someone had pulled him away from her. She opened her eyes just in time to see his brother deliver him a punishing blow to the jaw. Taken completely by surprise, Jared went down like a sack of potatoes, landing in a pile of straw and horse manure that had not yet been cleared away. Nursing bruised knuckles, Grady studied him for a moment, then hauled him up by the front of his jacket, angry enough to deliver another blow. Whether or not Jared was still unconscious, he had the sense to pretend he was out for the count.

'Leave him, Grady,' she managed to say at last. 'You've done enough.'

'But you're hurt.' Grady dropped Jared to the ground again and came to look at her. Frowning, he held a clean handkerchief to her bleeding lip.

'No, no. It looks worse than it is.' Alex mumbled, realizing the blow had also caused her to bite her tongue. 'He didn't have time to do much.'

'I ought to kill him for this. He can take his red Porsche and get out of here now. Today. I want him out of my life for good.'

Vere was the next person to arrive on the scene, quick to take in the sight of Jared, unconscious on the ground, and his daughter with spots of blood on her dress.

'My God, what happened here?' he said. 'Is he dead?'

'No such luck.' Grady smiled at the thought. 'He was attacking Alex so I had to knock him out.'

'I should've known something was wrong when you took so long to get ready this morning.' Vere said. 'Why didn't you confide in me?'

186

'Because I didn't know what I wanted to do, Dad,' she said in a small voice. 'It was only when I arrived and saw Jared—how angry he was because I was late—I just knew I couldn't go through with it.'

'No, Alex. I think there's a lot more to it than that,' Grady said. 'You need to tell us everything.'

And, haltingly, with her eyes cast down almost as if she were ashamed of her eavesdropping, she did.

Grady sighed, shaking his head when she finished her tale. 'I'm so sorry, Alex, I should've done something about it before. Jared was always a womanizer and just as shallow as his mother. I'm the biggest fool for thinking he'd changed.'

'It's my fault, too,' she said through her swollen lip. 'For a while there I had myself convinced that I was in love with him.'

'But not any more?' Grady studied her, waiting intently for her answer.

Alex shrugged.

'We need to get you out of here,' Grady said. 'I'll herd the wedding guests into the marquee and break out the champagne. That'll keep them busy. They've had a miserable morning and somebody's got to eat all that food. Vere can spirit you away while I'm doing it.'

'And what about—?' Vere indicated Jared who had not yet come round.

'These are my stables, my house and he's no

187

longer welcome here,' Grady said in a loud voice, fully aware that Jared could hear him. 'And if he comes anywhere near me, now or at any time in the future, I'll knock him down again.'

CHAPTER TEN

Jared sat up and felt carefully all around his jaw. Although it had to be severely bruised, nothing seemed to be broken and he was relieved to find he hadn't lost any teeth. From past experience he knew that his brother packed a wallop and realized he had got away lightly; at least there would be no permanent damage. Prudently, he had waited until everyone left before staggering to his feet, feeling groggy and brushing the worst of the muck and straw from his clothes. Outside, he could hear laughter and music as the party raged on inside the marquee. People were still prepared to enjoy themselves at a wedding party even minus the bride and groom.

Knowing better than to let anyone see him, Jared crept around the stables and made for his Porsche, pulling a face when he saw it had already been decorated for their departure as newlyweds. Using his Swiss Army knife, he severed the strings tying tin cans to the rear of the car, stripped away streamers of coloured toilet paper and burst the balloons. There was nothing he could do about 'Just Married' written on the rear window in white paint. He could only hope it would wash off.

Making as little noise as he could, he started the car and drove quietly away before the wedding guests realized he was leaving. He didn't want to see anyone or answer any awkward questions. He was leaving his brother's property for the last time and didn't mean to come back, even to pick up the things he had left behind. Apart from a few clothes in his old bedroom, his home theatre and everything else that he treasured had been transferred to his city apartment. The fortunate part about being wealthy was that anything and everything could be replaced without feeling the pinch—even girls.

He smiled to himself. He'd played a daring and ingenious game and if things had gone slightly differently, he would have won. But now he would do what he always did when he got into trouble—lie low at his mother's apartment in Queensland until the scandal blew over.

He didn't call her until he stopped to buy petrol and food at a big roadside service station, making sure he was sitting at a table well away from the general hubbub and where he wouldn't be overheard.

'Well?' He heard his mother's faintly mocking tone when she picked up her phone in Queensland. 'How's my son the married man?' It had been a bone of contention between them that Simone refused to return to Melbourne for the wedding. She disapproved of her son's choice and didn't care who knew it.

'I'm not married, Ma. She dumped me at the altar.'

'Sensible girl!' Simone chuckled richly. 'And don't tell me you're heartbroken because I won't believe it. I know you better than anyone. Hold on while I find my ciggies and refresh my drink. I'm going to enjoy this.' Simone was gone for about a minute. 'Sitting comfortably now. So tell me, what happened? What did you do to put her off?'

'Nothing much. Except yesterday I screwed her best friend while she was away at her father's place. Somehow she must've found out.'

'They always find out—the best friend would make sure of it, anyway.' Simone lit a cigarette and he heard her inhaling deeply. 'It is a bit much, Jared, even for you. Betraying your bride on the eve of the wedding.'

'It was nothing, Ma. I know guys who've had pole dancers at their bucks' nights. Never hear any complaints about that.'

'Because it's not personal, is it? Not the same as having a fling with the best friend.'

'But it didn't mean anything. Not to me.'

'I know that. But women see things

190

differently.'

'Well, you weren't here to advise me, were you?'

Simone sighed, bored now that Jared was starting to whine. 'I never understood what you saw in Alexis, anyway. Great gawk of a girl. Nothing of the lady about her. I always thought you could do better than that.'

'Maybe I will now. As the boy wonder—the new CEO of Allen Enterprises. Besides, don't most women like a man with a past?'

'Don't trip over that ego, will you?' Simone giggled. 'You'd better come up here for a week or so till the fuss dies down. There's something I want to discuss with you—but not over the phone. I have a wealthy friend who needs a new partner. You might even think of transferring your business interests up here.'

'Sounds good to me. I can leave the lovely Olivia to take care of the Melbourne end.'

'See you soon, then.'

'I knew I could rely on you to come up with something. Thanks, Ma.'

'And stop calling me Ma. It makes me feel about a hundred.'

He snapped the phone shut, grinning. He finished off his 'all day breakfast' and returned to the Porsche, surprised to see a girl waiting beside it.

He recognized Katrina, still wearing the clothes she had worn in the stables and with a bulging canvas bag at her feet. Somehow he knew it contained all she had in the world. Uncertain of her welcome under his stony gaze, she looked windblown and slightly grubby after her travels, anxiously biting her lip.

'I thought I'd catch up with you here.' She said, trying to smile. 'It's the only café for miles. I hitched a ride.'

'So I see.' Jared was in no mood to be gentle. 'Well, you can hitch another one and take yourself home again. You're not coming with me.'

'Please, Jared.' She was becoming plaintive. 'I've left Allens and everyone must know what happened by now. I can't go back.'

'Not my problem. I didn't ask you to follow me. To be honest, Kat, you're beginning to bore me. You're not that crash hot in bed.'

'We haven't made love in a bed.'

He snapped his fingers. 'Oh, that's right. I was thinking of somebody else.'

Tears stood in her eyes as she stared at him. 'I never knew you could be so heartless. So cruel,' she whispered.

'Ah well, you live and learn.' He gave her a mocking salute, popped the doors of his car and jumped into the driver's seat.

'Jared, please.' She glanced around nervously as she realized what a mistake it had been to follow him. People were watching them now. 'You can't leave me stranded like this. At least drop me somewhere I can—'

'Sorry.' He cut short her protests. 'Got a lot of road to cover before nightfall.'

'Jared, you have to help me. I don't have much money.' She made one last attempt to get into the car only to find he had locked all the doors against her. 'Please—please take me with you.'

'Not this time, sweets.' He opened the window just sufficiently to speak to her. 'An' if I were you, I'd have a wash an' brush up before trying to hitch another ride.'

So saying, he winked at her before taking off at speed, deliberately raising dust, and leaving her blinking and coughing in the exhaust fumes from his car.

*   *   *

Remorse kicked in a few miles down the track. Katrina had unsettled him by turning up so unexpectedly, but he knew he had been unnecessarily unkind and mean. He had used her shamefully and should have had the decency to take her to a bus or train station and made sure she had enough money to get home. He had been travelling fast and saw that he had put fifty kilometres on the clock since he left her behind but an exit was fast coming up. It was now or never, he told himself. Forget Kat and continue his journey, or do the right thing and turn back?

Making a quick decision, he took the exit

and quickly returned the way he had come. If she was no longer there, then he would have nothing to worry about and his conscience would be clear. At the speeds he travelled, he would have wasted only half an hour.

He returned to the service complex, cursing himself for a sentimental fool and fully expecting to find her gone. But there she was, exactly where he had left her, slumped on the ground beside her old canvas bag, her knees drawn up and her head buried in her arms. She looked totally defeated and he couldn't tell if she was weeping or not.

He drew up beside her and leaned over to open the passenger's door. 'All right, you win. Hurry up and get in,' he snapped, still unable to be gracious.

She raised a tear-stained face to glare at him. 'Go away, Jared,' she muttered. 'I know you don't want me. You've made that more than clear.'

'Get in,' he said. 'Or do I have to get out and throw you into the car?'

She wrestled her canvas bag into the small space behind the seats and then climbed into the passenger's seat beside him, smelling of stale sweat and tears, still shaken by the occasional shuddering sob.

'Ah, get over yourself, Kat.' He glanced at the unsavoury specimen seated beside him before driving off. 'Don't take it so much to heart. You know I didn't mean all those things

194

I said.'

'Oh, I think you did,' she said softly. 'It's maybe the first time you've told me the truth. Why did you come back?'

He shrugged. 'I wouldn't like to think of you cadging a lift with a maniac and ending up dead in a ditch.'

She blew her nose and smiled ruefully. 'There aren't as many maniacs around as most people think. Everyone took care to ignore me.'

'All right.' Suddenly, he was all business. 'Where do you want me to take you?'

'I don't know,' she said listlessly. 'I didn't think of anything except catching up with you. Where are *you* going?'

'To visit my mother in Queensland and, before you ask, the answer's no. I'm not taking you with me. My ma would have a pink fit.'

Her lip trembled and her eyes filled with tears again.

'Oh, God, don't start that again,' he said. 'I'll drop you at the next town where there's a bus or a rail station so you can get home.'

'OK.' She tried to smile through her misery, realizing this was the best offer she was going to get.

Jared drove swiftly, enjoying the smooth running of his powerful car. Conversation lapsed for a while until he realized Katrina was studying him intently, stretching one arm behind him across the back of his seat.

'What is it now? What?' he said, trying not to show the irritation he felt. Her body odour was rank and he now wished conscience hadn't got the better of him and that he had left her behind.

'Tell me, Jared,' she asked in a small voice, 'did you ever love me? Even a little bit?'

He rolled his eyes and groaned. 'Why do girls always do this? You want to analyse everything, confusing love with the simple matter of lust. You knew we could never be more than a one-night stand because I was marrying Alex—'

'You never spelled it out like that before. And anyway, you didn't marry her, did you?'

'You have it the wrong way round: it was Alex who didn't get married to me.'

'But I love you, Jared! Really I do. I could be so much more for you than she could— more than you ever dreamed.' And, even as they were travelling at this high speed, she moved across, trying to press herself into his arms.

'Get off me while I'm driving!' Jared yelled. She was making him nervous now. They had been doing almost 100 k.p.h. and she was blocking his vision. He couldn't see where he was going. 'You'll have us off the road in a moment.'

'I don't care.' She was breathing heavily now and getting hysterical. 'I'd rather die with you now, today, than go on living without you.'

She started wrenching the wheel, trying to pull the car out of control and into a skid.

With death staring him in the face, Jared didn't hesitate for a second. Hoping the car would stay on course for a moment or two, he seized Katrina by the hair with his left hand before using the right to give her a punishing blow to the face. Dizzy and almost unconscious, she let go of the wheel and leaned back in her seat, trying to stem the flow of blood from her nose.

Able to see again, he brought the car under control and pulled into a convenient lay-by with emergency phones. That was a close call and he was badly shaken.

Furious with her now, he jumped out, and threw out her canvas bag to land on the road.

'Jared, don't do this.' She could hardly speak with the blood still pouring from her nose. 'You can't leave me out here on the open road.'

'I'm done with you, crazy bitch. You could have killed us both.'

'I'm sorry. I didn't mean—'

'Get out now! You're bleeding all over my car.' Roughly, he came and dragged her out of it, trying not to look at her face which was a mess of tears and blood. This was the last time he would play the Good Samaritan. Getting back into the driver's seat, he grimaced as he saw there was blood on the passenger seat and on the floor of the car as well as a residual smell of Katrina's sweat. It would need valet cleaning as soon as he could arrange it. He climbed back in and drove off swiftly without a backward glance. So far as he was concerned, Katrina was gone from his life— forever. Perhaps now he could continue his journey without event.

Half an hour later he heard a siren behind him and looked in the mirror to see a highway patrol car coming up fast behind him with blue and red lights flashing overhead. It drew level and the policemen signalled for him to pull over and stop. He swore under his breath. He was sure he hadn't been speeding but experience had taught him that a new Porsche was always a target for the law.

The police car angled in front of him, forcing him to a stand-still and not one but both policemen got out and came over to speak to him, settling the guns on their hips and adjusting their caps.

'What's wrong, Officer?' He leaned out, trying to seem casual as if he hadn't a care in the world. 'I was obeying the speed limits, wasn't I?'

'Driver's licence and registration, please.' The older man spoke but both officers were looking grim and in no mood to be coerced.

'There's my driver's licence.' He handed it over. 'For obvious reasons I don't keep the registration papers in the car. If it were to be stolen—'

The younger policeman took no notice of what he was saying but peered into the car, quick to register the smears of blood on the passenger seat and on the floor. He raised his eyebrows significantly at his older colleague.

Seconds later, Jared found himself cautioned, cuffed and on his way to the nearest police station. 'Please,' he asked them, more scared than he had ever been in his life, 'what have I done? Aren't you going to tell me what this is about?'

'We're not obliged to tell you anything until you are charged, sir.' The older officer looked at him through narrowed eyes. 'But I'll give you something to think about. A young lady has made some very serious complaints against you. And I have every sympathy with her—I have a daughter about her age.'

'Katrina,' Jared murmured, closing his eyes and sinking back in his seat. She must have taken revenge by inventing some lies. 'But hey—what about my car? Can't I drive it to the station and meet you there?'

The policemen looked at each other and laughed as if he had made a very funny joke. 'We'll arrange for it to be towed,' the younger one said. 'You might find you're going to be with us for some time.'

*　　　*　　　*

Around six o'clock that same evening Grady's

mobile rang. He glanced at it and was irritated to see that the caller was Jared. What could he possibly want from him now? He considered refusing to take the call but he knew Jared was capable of pestering all night if need be. All the same, he was terse. He didn't want his brother to think himself so easily forgiven.

'Yes, Jared. What do you want?'

'Oh, Grady, thank God.'

'I'll give you thirty seconds.'

'No, no, Grady, please. Please don't hang up. I'm in trouble here and they'll only allow me to make one call.'

'That sounds as if you're with the Police. I should leave you to stew in your own juice after what you did. So why are you in trouble now, Bro?'

'Nothing. Well, not much anyway. Katrina's telling them I tried to rape her and beat her up.'

'And did you?'

'No! Well, not the rape bit, anyway. She was hysterical—trying to wreck the car and kill us by leaning across and wrenching the steering wheel. I had to hit her to make her stop. You have to believe me.'

'Oddly enough, I do. Rape isn't your style. So where are you?'

'I dunno. Some hick town just over the border in New South Wales.'

'That kind of talk won't make you too many friends. Find out where you are exactly and I'll come up. Might take me a couple of hours, though.'

'Thank you, Bro.'

'And what's happened to Katrina? Where is she now? Do you know?'

'They're not likely to tell me, are they?'

'OK.' Grady sighed with resignation. 'Just sit tight and I'll be there as soon as I can.'

'As if I have any choice. They're not going to let me go anywhere. Thanks, Bro.'

*   *   *

Grady arrived to find that it was indeed a small country town with a pub on each corner of most of the main streets. The police station was prominent and Grady saw there were one or two down-at-heel motels. Before alerting the police to his presence, he decided to check out the motels first. Although the first one drew a blank, he ran Katrina to earth in the second; a subdued Katrina, sporting puffy eyes and some large band-aids over her nose.

'I don't want to upset you, Katrina, but can I come in?' he asked.

Shrugging, she opened the door and went to turn off the television. It was noisy with people screaming with joy at the outcome of a game show.

'Sit down,' She said, indicating the only chair, and flopping back on the bed.

'Nasty.' He peered at her nose which looked

as if it was broken. 'Did Jared do that?'

Miserably, she nodded.

'Tell me how it happened.'

Reluctantly, she explained that Jared had taunted her and how she had tried to steer them into the oncoming traffic and that he had to hit her to regain control of the car.

'Yes and what happened when he finally stopped. Was that when he tried to rape you?'

She stared at him, looking frightened, and whispered, 'Actually, no. I was angry and wanted to get him into even more trouble. So I made it up.'

'Katrina, I need you to come to the police station with me right now and tell them exactly what you have told me.'

'I can't,' she said. 'They were so kind and sympathetic. I can't go back to them now and say it was all a lie.'

'I think you have to. I can see that you're hurt. Jared shouldn't have hit you and I'm sure he's sorry for it now—'

Katrina gave a snort of disbelief and then winced as it hurt her nose.

'But the charge of rape is a much more serious one and would have to be proved. People are going to ask you a lot more questions and you'll have a medical examination—'

'When they'll find out that nothing happened.' She was ahead of him there. 'All right, Grady, I'll do it. 'Long as I don't have to

202

see Jared again.'

The policemen had little excitement in their small country town and were disappointed when Katrina told them that the more serious charges would have to be dropped. And they believed Grady when he told them his brother struck out at Katrina to stop her wrecking the car and most likely killing them both.

An hour later, Jared had been released and was ready to resume his journey north.

'I can't thank you enough, Bro,' he said. 'You came and saved me. I feel pretty rotten now after what I did to you.'

'Why?' Grady said slowly. 'What did you do?'

'Alex.'

Grady tensed. 'What about her?'

Jared sighed. 'Sometimes I don't know why I do all these things. I just do them because I can. I could see you were interested in her right from the start—at that birthday party of hers. So I just had to get in there first. I was even ready to marry her to keep her from you.'

'Just be grateful you never told me any of this before.' Grady could feel a simmering anger just underneath the surface. 'And don't ask me for a favour ever again. I want you to get in that car and put as much distance between us as possible. And from now on stay the hell out of my way.'

'I did say I was sorry.'

'No, you didn't. You just said you felt pretty rotten about what you'd done.'

'I don't want us to part bad friends, Bro.'

'I think it's a little late for that.'

Also Grady was in no mood to be gracious to Katrina when he left the police station to find her standing beside his car.

'What now?' he said.

'I just wanted to thank you.' She was speaking scarcely above a whisper. 'And I wondered if—if you'd take me back to Cranbourne? If I could have my job back?'

'I don't think so, Katrina. Not after all that's happened. I'll see that your wages are paid up to date and I'll give you two weeks' severance. But that's as far as I'm prepared to go.'

Katrina studied him for a moment. 'You want her to come back, don't you? Alex, I mean?'

He could see no point in denying it. 'I really hope so.'

Katrina smiled. 'You're in love with her yourself, aren't you?'

He frowned. 'Don't be ridiculous. I'm a friend of her father.'

'Since when did that stop anyone?'

'Look,' he said, desperate to change the subject and reaching for his wallet. 'Here's a hundred dollars. Is that enough to get you back to your family or somewhere safe?'

'Oh, yes,' she said, grasping it eagerly. 'You can deduct it from my wages.'

'No, keep it.'

'Thanks.'

After that, there wasn't much else to say. Grady went to a service station to fill up his Mercedes and then he drove slowly home. One way and another, he had a lot to think about.

CHAPTER ELEVEN

At Wonga Park, Mim wasn't all that delighted to see her stepdaughter home. Instead of marrying a wealthy man and leaving Vere to establish his new family and get on with his life, here she was home again, occupying her old room and spending most of her time in there—the room Mim had hoped to redecorate for the coming child.

'I don't know what Alex was thinking of,' she grumbled to Vere when they were alone. 'Turning down a wonderful catch like that.'

'Not so wonderful, after all. He hit her and split her lip.'

Mim shrugged. 'Well, you can't say he wasn't provoked. She kept him waiting for over an hour and then dumped him at the altar. My sympathies are with Jared.'

'Well, keep your opinions to yourself,' Vere said. 'You don't know the whole story and I'm not about to tell you.'

205

'Why not? I'm your wife. It's not fair for you to keep secrets from me.'

'Because they're not *my* secrets.' Vere wasn't to be pressed. 'It's up to Alex. If she wants to confide in you, no doubt she will.'

'That's likely, isn't it?' Mim gave a derisive snort. 'So how long is she going to hang around here moping?'

'I don't know. She's my daughter, Miriam and this is her family home—she will stay as long as she likes.'

'All right. So I'll have to turn that back room into a nursery. It's too small and it hardly gets any sunlight. Not the ideal place to bring up a baby.'

'I'm sure it's only temporary, Mim. Try to have a little patience.' Vere sighed. Even as he said this, he knew that his wife's patience was in very short supply.

And Mim wasn't the only one to side with Jared. Jen was equally put out by what she saw as her cousin's crazy behaviour when they met for coffee in Jen's lunch-hour a week or so later. Alex thought she owed her bridesmaid some sort of explanation, but Jennifer launched an attack without waiting to hear it.

'I don't know what's wrong with you,' she complained. 'You had it all in the palm of your hand—a good-looking husband and loaded with it as well—and what do you do? Change your mind at the last minute and throw it all away. If you can't spare a thought for yourself, think of me. I'll get nada! No hope of meeting his soldier-friend now.'

'You never did have any hope of meeting him.' Alex fired back at her. She'd had quite enough of everyone taking Jared's part. 'Jared was awfully good at making promises he wouldn't bother to keep.'

'I still can't understand what went so wrong.'

Alex paused for a moment; then she took a quick breath and told her the truth. On some level it pleased her that, as she described Jared's perfidy, Jen's eyes widened and she slumped further and further into her chair, gaping like a fish. 'On the very day before we were to be married,' Alex concluded. 'So you can close your mouth now because that's all there is.'

It took Jennifer several seconds to find her voice. 'Alex, I'm so sorry. And all the things I said to you. I'm sorry—I had no idea.' She considered it for a moment, absorbing what she had heard. 'But why didn't you call off the wedding at once as soon as you found him out? Why continue with the charade?'

'I was in shock, I suppose. I didn't want to believe my own eyes. I needed my world to remain the nice, safe place I always thought it was.'

'So what are you going to do now? Do you still have your job at the stables?'

Alex shrugged. 'I don't know. That depends on Grady. I'll have to wait and see.'

Jen glanced at her watch and pulled a face. 'Sorry! I'll have to go. I've already had a warning for taking too long at lunch. You keep in touch Alex.' She sprang to her feet, but another thought made her pause before leaving. 'And don't stay too long with that poisonous Mim. She's enough to depress anyone. I'll be sorry for that baby of hers.'

Alex smiled, feeling no other answer was necessary. At least now she had an ally in Jen.

*   *   *

And then she answered the front door of her father's house late one afternoon to find Grady Allen standing there. For a moment neither said anything and then they both smiled and spoke at the same time.

'Oh, Alex—'

'Grady, I—no, you first—'

'Can I come in? It's a bit damp out here.' He indicated the drizzling, grey skies overhead.

'Of course. What am I thinking of?' She ushered him in the direction of Vere's study. 'If you're looking for Dad, he's not here. Taking Mim to the hospital for an ultrasound.'

'No, Alex. I came to see you.' He took the seat she offered and looked around the room, admiring the silver cups on the shelves together with the many photographic records of Vere's success. 'Madge is really missing you. Tasha's done a wonderful job looking after

208

her but, at this time of year and with the Carnival almost upon us, I need her to spend more time with the other horses. I wondered if you feel up to returning to work yet?'

'You want me to come back? After all that has happened and what I did?'

'Why not?' The question appeared to surprise him. 'What happened between you and Jared wasn't *your* fault.'

'Not everyone's going to see it that way.' She was hesitant. 'And then there's Katrina. I can't share a room with her—not any more. There have been too many harsh words between us.'

'That won't be necessary. Katrina's gone. She left at the same time as Jared.'

'He took her with him?' Alex was surprised to find such a thought didn't hurt her at all.

'No. She followed him. It didn't turn out well.' He considered saying no more, but she was watching him expectantly so, quickly and succinctly, he told her what had happened on the road. 'And that's absolutely the last time I put my hand up to haul him out of trouble,' he concluded. 'If Jared runs true to form, he'll join up with his mother and hide out on the Gold Coast for a while till the fuss dies down. Simone has always loved having time alone with her son.'

She nodded. 'Yes, I know. She can be very—'

'Possessive.' Grady supplied the word. 'She would have been the mother in-law from hell. You have no idea what a lucky escape you've had.'

Alex grinned. 'I'm beginning to. And of course I'll come back. I've missed everyone so much. Toby and Tasha—and Madge of course.' She was too shy to mention that she had missed him, too. 'With Katrina gone, there's no reason I shouldn't. When do you want me to start?'

'No time like the present. I can give you a lift. Unless you prefer to drive your own car?'

'No. It's being serviced at present and won't be ready till next week. Can you give me a few minutes to pack my bags?'

'Take as long as you need. And put on a dress. I'm buying you dinner on the way home. We're long overdue.'

'You don't have to do that, Grady.' She bit her lip, remembering that each time Grady had asked her to dinner before, Jared had got in first.

'No, but I'd like to.'

She smiled, telling herself not to read too much into it. It wasn't a new thing—this pull of attraction towards Grady—but Jared had prevented her taking it further, never giving her time to think. She told herself not to be a romantic fool. Grady was just being kind and probably only wanted to talk of his plans for Madge.

She made coffee and left him to read a newspaper while she went upstairs to pack.

Then she searched her wardrobe for something to wear, not wanting to choose anything she had worn on a date with Jared. Finally, she put on the burgundy chiffon—her birthday dress. Then she added a black Spanish shawl that had belonged to her mother, hoping it wouldn't be over the top for a simple dinner out.

Grady heard her bumping bags down the stairs and came to help out. He carried them outside and loaded them into the boot of his Mercedes while she left a note for her father in the hall.

'That's the dress you wore to your birthday party. I always thought how well it suited you,' he said, almost uncomfortable delivering the compliment.

'Fancy you remembering that.' She said. 'I hope it isn't too much—?'

'Not at all. I want to take you to a favourite place of mine—it's at the top of the tallest building—they call it the highest dining experience in the Southern hemisphere.'

'Oh, no.' She slumped against the car, remembering the vertigo she had felt as the lift rocketed skywards and how Jared had laughed at her fears. 'I'm sorry Grady, but I can't—'

'It's OK. You don't have to tell me. You went there with Jared?'

She nodded, miserable at disappointing him.

'Forget the tower. There's a Chinese place I know where the food is to die for—'

'Not the Golden something or other, halfway down Little Bourke Street?'

'That's the one. But let me guess. You went there with Jared, too?'

Once more she nodded.

'I should've murdered the little brute when I had the chance.' Grady laughed. 'He's taken you to all of my favourite places.'

'And mine! I took him to my favourite fish and chip shop at the beach.'

He put his head in his hands and groaned in mock horror.

'Grady, it doesn't matter.' She laughed rather wildly. 'Melbourne has scores of wonderful restaurants. We can find somewhere else.' In the end they discovered a tiny French bistro on a side street in South Yarra. It was so newly opened, the white paint was scarcely dry on the walls and what they could see of the kitchen gleamed with new stainless steel. The menu was traditional French fare and, as soon as they were seated, they were treated to complimentary drinks to celebrate the owners' first week of operation, together with hot, home made bread rolls.

It belonged to a young French couple who seemed shy and unused to being in the public eye. They explained that this was their first venture into the restaurant business. The husband prepared the meals while his pretty, young wife dealt with the front of the house. There was only one other person, a waitress, who came to advise them on the 'specials' and take their order.

While they waited for their garlic prawns to arrive, Grady spoke with enthusiasm, bringing Alex up to date with his plans for Madge's Spring Carnival campaign.

'It depends if she can win another mare's race first.' He said. 'There's a night meeting at Moonee Valley and I've got her booked into that. Even if she wins, I don't think she'll be up for any of the major events but she should be able to snag one or two of the minor prizes. It's the noise of the crowd that still troubles her most.'

'Maybe if she wore blinkers, she wouldn't be so scared,' Alex suggested.

'And maybe she'll freak out still more if she can't see what's going on around her. It's still a question of trial and error I'm afraid.'

'I don't want anything bad to happen to her.'

'No, nor do I.' He said, taking her hand across the table. 'Not after we saved her for the second time and she's been doing so well. I never realized, Alex, that anyone could care for her as much as I do.'

'She was precious to me from the moment I saw her and we took to each other at once.'

Their meals arrived at that moment and they gave their full attention to the deliciously spicy food. When they were finished, Grady ordered a whisky to finish off his meal while Alex told him she'd prefer coffee.

'Alex'—he sat back, regarding her—'there's something I need to say. I don't want to give you the wrong impression. I'm not at all like my brother. I didn't ask you out tonight so that I could come on to you later.'

'Oh no,' she said quickly and felt herself blushing. 'I didn't think that for a moment. Of course not.'

'You must still be so hurt, so betrayed by what Jared has done, you'll need some time to recover. I'd like to give you that time. Working with Magenta will give you a different focus. And when—when you do fall in love again as I'm sure you will—'

Alex frowned. 'It's too soon, Grady. I can't think about that.'

'I know. But you're young and resilient.' He was determined to have his say. 'And when you do fall in love, it won't be with someone like me of your father's generation—'

'But you're much younger than Dad. And I've never thought of you as a father figure. Not at all.' Having made her speech, she laughed a little nervously, unsure where this conversation was leading. She didn't want Grady to be discouraged, but she could scarcely say she had fallen out of love with Jared on the day he betrayed her. In hindsight she could see their romance had never been real—at no time had there been any connection of souls. Her heart remained undamaged and whole, completely her own.

214

But how could she say so? Grady would think her a shallow person indeed to fall in and out of love so easily.

'What I'm trying to say and making a total hash of it'—Grady stared into the bottom of his whisky glass—'is that you have nothing to fear from me. If you were thinking—after that time I kissed you in Toby's office—'

'Oh, that? Never gave it a moment's thought. I can scarcely remember it,' she said airily, hoping it didn't sound like a lie.

'Good. Because it was a silly mistake. It won't happen again.'

'Grady,' she said slowly, wondering how to get him down from the superior position of 'older man' and open up to her, 'why is it that you've never married?'

The stiffening of his back should have warned her she had strayed on to dangerous ground. 'What makes you ask that?'

'Is it because you push people away before they can get close to you?'

'I don't,' he muttered, but Alex chose to ignore the warning signs and pressed on.

'You shouldn't be so hard on yourself. Jared told me what happened—that you lost the girl you loved. But that was a long time ago now and—'

'What did he tell you? What?' Grady's mood had changed completely, making Alex recoil from the fierceness of his expression. 'I never speak about it. Jared knows that.'

215

'It was nothing, really.' She said in a small voice, wishing she'd never opened this particular can of worms. 'Just that you were supposed to marry this girl and she died. He didn't even know how.'

'He should know better than to gossip about me.' Grady was not to be appeased. 'And besides, he knows nothing about it. He was only a child.'

'I'm sorry. I only mentioned it because I wanted to understand.'

'Well, you can forget it. Because there's no need.'

'I think there is, Grady, or you wouldn't still be so angry about it.'

'I don't want to discuss it, Alex. Now or at any other time. The subject is closed.'

She shrugged, wishing her curiosity hadn't led her down this path. She'd had no idea it would ruin what had been an otherwise perfect evening.

He stood up, signalling to their waitress that he wanted the check. 'I expect you're tired, Alex. It's selfish of me to keep you out so late. I think it's time we went home.'

And, although she hoped for an opportunity to steer the conversation along a different path, he turned up the music on the radio and gave her no chance to speak as he joined the busy freeway and drove back to Cranbourne.

*　　*　　*

216

In spite of Grady distancing himself once again, Alex settled back into her routine with Madge as if she had never been away. The main difference was in the way the other hands treated her. Mike and the lads were consistently cheerful and kind but the other girls—who had treated her like some kind of high-school princess who made them all jealous—now accepted her into their circle as if they had always been friends. More than one of them had been badly treated by Jared and they respected her decision to jilt him at the altar, thinking it was no more than he deserved. Alex returned to the room she had shared with Katrina but, so far, Mrs Brookes had allowed her to occupy it on her own. Everyone seemed to realize that she needed some space and time on her own. Occasionally, when she was alone in the room they had shared, she wondered why Katrina had seen fit to betray her and where she was now. She couldn't help feeling that things hadn't turned out well.

*   *   *

Madge was taken to the night meeting in a float on her own with Mike to drive and Alex to reassure her and keep her calm. After the unhappy experience of riding in a big float with other horses, Grady had decided that this was the best way to move her. After a lot of thought and discussion, Tash persuaded them to let her race one more time without blinkers.

The evening crowd was small but fairly rowdy and Alex spoke encouragingly, keeping a firm hold on Magenta as they paraded, prior to giving her into Tasha's care. The race for fillies and mares was only the second on the programme and, afterwards, they would be free to go home. The field was small and evenly matched; Tasha thought they had a very good chance of winning, so long as nothing happened to upset the excitable filly.

Entry into the stalls went smoothly and Tasha was unconcerned that they had an outside gate. That would enable her to hang back and keep Madge out of trouble during the early stages of the race and she felt sure the big filly would find the necessary turn of speed to come round the outside and win when they reached the straight.

As Alex and Grady watched, the race went entirely according to plan and Magenta Magic came up the centre of the course to emerge a clear winner by more than two lengths. On the way back to scale, Tasha stood up in the saddle and grinned, waving at them triumphantly.

Then everything went wrong.

Fireworks that the racing club had planned to explode when the racing was over were set off too early, even before the jockeys returned

218

to scale. Accompanied by shrill whistles and muffled bangs, colourful star-bursts and cascades tore across the sky, sputtering as they fell back to earth. Madge and several other young horses reared in fright. Fortunately, most of the jockeys were able to bring their mounts under control. All except Tasha. Too thrilled with her win to realize at first that there might be a problem, she found herself flying through the air to fall awkwardly against the fence. There was a gasp of horrified surprise from the watching crowd.

As paramedics rushed on to the course to treat the injured girl, two clerks set off in pursuit of Magenta. Sensing freedom and full of herself because of her victory, Madge gave them a run for their money and completed a whole circuit of the course before they caught up with her. And when one of them reached out for her reins, she attempted to bite. She remained free until Grady and Alex were allowed to go on the course and catch her, behaving as if she knew very well how much trouble she had caused and was even amused by it.

Although Tasha needed to go to hospital with a suspected broken ankle and cracked ribs, preventing her going through the process of weighing in, it had been a decisive win and, to everyone's relief, the stewards allowed her to keep it.

On the way home, Mike and Alex fell into a

gloomy discussion.

'So who's goin' to ride her now?' Mike said. 'Tasha's going to be out of the picture for the Spring Carnival.'

'We don't know that for sure. Could be just a sprain,' Alex muttered. She didn't like the idea of introducing Madge to another jockey at this late stage.

'They wouldn't 'ave took her to the hospital if it was only a sprain. I'd ask Grady to let me ride her but—'

'Don't be daft—you're too heavy. You only ride track work—like me.'

'Won't be easy to find another girl now. All the good ones will be booked for most of the Carnival already.'

'You are a little ray of sunshine, aren't you? We don't know for sure that Tasha can't ride.'

Mike pulled a gloomy face, shaking his head.

*   *   *

The next day Grady and Alex went to see Tasha in hospital. She was sitting up in bed looking pale with a cage over her plastered foot.

'Look at that,' she grumbled. 'A clean break, they say. It hurts like hell and I might not be back in the saddle till after Christmas. I'm so sorry, Grady.'

'Not your fault,' he said, passing her a

basket of fruit and a big bunch of flowers. 'Blame those idiots for letting off fireworks. You ought to sue them, Tash.'

'And what good would that do? We'd just line the pockets of our respective lawyers. No thanks.' Tasha wrinkled her nose. 'It leaves you in a bit of a spot, though, doesn't it? I've been racking my brains to think of a rider for you—'

'And?' Grady said eagerly.

'I just might have one—she's a bit older than me—a senior rider when I was just starting out. She's Paige Sandford now. But you might remember her riding as Paige Warrender?'

'Yes, I do. In fact we were teenagers together. You can't hang around race tracks and horses without getting to know the other kids Her grandmother used to train horses, too. A stylish old lady. French.'

'That's the one.' Tasha started to write down some phone numbers. 'Now, I can't promise you'll do any good. Paige had a baby last year and I haven't seen her for some time. She might have got fat as butter and given up professional riding for good.'

'No harm in asking, is there?' Grady accepted Tasha's card with the phone numbers on the back. 'Thanks, Tash.'

Paige wouldn't make any promises over the phone, but she remembered Grady and invited him to call and see her at her home on the coast. Grady, in turn, asked Alex to make the trip with him although she took care to keep the conversation light and not drift on to dangerous grounds as before.

When Paige answered the door, they could see at once she had kept her whippet-like figure and not run to fat. She looked radiantly happy, as well. Impulsively, she embraced Alex and shook hands with the more conservative Grady.

'This is exciting, isn't it? I haven't had a ride in the Spring Carnival for some time.' She tossed her unruly fair hair, inviting them to follow her down to the farmhouse kitchen. 'Although I don't like to profit from Tasha's misfortune. How's she doing, by the way?'

'Oh, you know,' Alex shrugged. 'Fed up and wishing it hadn't happened.'

The kitchen proved to be an unusually large family room, dominated by a massive dining table surrounded by comfortable chairs and a huge dresser decorated with antique china. The room was fragrant with bunches of herbs which hung from the ceiling and Alex closed her eyes, breathing deeply to enjoy their rich scent. It was the kind of kitchen you see in old French films.

A brooding, dark-haired man stood arms folded and with his back to the huge kitchen stove. Paige introduced him as her husband, Luke, and he didn't look pleased to see them.

'I'll say at the outset that I'm not too keen on this,' he said. 'I've heard all about your filly

222

and some people say she's nothing but trouble.'

'For goodness' sake, Luke.' Paige flicked him on the shoulder. 'Let us at least hear them out and then I'll decide for myself. Make yourself useful and pour us some drinks. Gin and tonic all round?'

'Not for me,' Alex said quickly. 'I'll take orange juice if you have any, thanks.'

They sat around the kitchen table and Paige served hot, home-made cheese straws to go with the drinks. They were delicious and served to lighten the mood.

'Look,' Grady said at last, 'we're in a hole here. If I don't get a jockey for Madge on Emirates' Stakes Day, we'll have to scratch.'

'So scratch.' Luke shrugged. 'It won't be the end of the world.'

'No, but it'll take us another twelve months to bring Madge back into top racing condition as she is now. It could even be the end of her career.'

Alex gasped. This was the first she'd heard of it. But Grady held up a hand for her to be silent.

'OK,' he said. 'I do understand your concerns, Luke. I'm not trying to belittle them, or push Paige into something against her will—'

'I wouldn't let you do that.' Luke said, aggressively protective towards his wife.

'Oh, do stop it, Luke.' Paige flicked him

again. 'This opportunity might be my last and I'll wonder about it forever, if I don't try.'

'But it isn't just you we have to think about, is it? You're a mother now, Paige. What am I going to tell Marc and Celia if you end up dead?'

'I'm not going to end up dead.' Paige rolled her eyes, shaking her head. 'Look, I don't think we can make this decision tonight,' she said at last. 'Let me come to Cranbourne and look at this filly of yours—'

'Yes, and I'm coming with you, if you do,' Luke growled, making Paige sigh and close her eyes. It was nice to be cherished but sometimes she wished he wasn't quite so possessive.

'May I say something?' Alex ventured, although she was shy to speak up in front of Luke whose dislike of the project was all too apparent.

'Sure,' Paige said. 'You're her strapper and must know her better than anyone. Go ahead.'

'For a start, Madge is highly strung, but she isn't really ill-natured. It's only when something goes wrong that she takes fright—'

'And can you guarantee that won't happen when my wife's on her back?' Luke was quick to break in. 'Things go wrong on the racecourse all the time.'

'As I've already said'—Paige glared at her husband—'we can't make this decision tonight. I need to see her for myself. And, if

224

we like each other, and feel we can work together, you need look no further. You've got your new rider.'

'Thank you, Paige.' Grady clasped her hand to seal the bargain. 'How soon can you come over to see her?'

'Tomorrow.' Paige grinned, jabbing her husband in the ribs. He was still ruining his good looks with a scowl. 'And, if you insist on being there, you can keep your mouth shut, Luke. I'll make this decision alone.'

Luke shrugged but he didn't argue further.

*   *   *

Paige was as good as her word, arriving at Cranbourne when all the horses had been hosed down after work but the hands had not yet left for their mid-morning break. Surprisingly, after all he had said, Luke had allowed her to visit alone.

'Crisis in the office,' she answered Grady's querying look. 'At least *he* thinks there is. I had a word with his PA. We'll reach a decision more easily without him pouring contempt on it.'

Using the same technique with Madge that she had employed with Tasha, Alex allowed Magenta to walk between them before letting Paige get up to ride. There was such an instant rapport between Madge and her new rider that Alex felt almost a pang of jealousy

225

as Paige rode the excitable filly as if she had always been part of her life. Grady watched them, leaning against the fence and chewing a stalk of grass.

'She's a beauty, all right.' Paige patted Madge she jumped off and walked towards Grady. 'Plenty of spirit, too. She reminds me of my grandmother's horse, Pierette.'

'The Caulfield Cup winner?' Alex remembered seeing the race and its surprise winner.

'That's the one. But we had to retire her after that.'

'Well?' Grady could scarcely contain his impatience, waiting to hear Paige's decision.

'I'll take the ride on Emirates' Stakes Day— of course I will. I have no problem with her. She's a beautiful girl.'

'Thank you!' Grady almost ran towards Toby's office with his mobile already at his ear. He wanted to give the good news to Toby at once and had several important phone calls to make.

Alex watched him leave, looking thoughtful as they put Madge's coat on and led her back to her stable. 'Paige,' she said, 'you should know what you're getting into here. Madge isn't quite the same on race day as she is at home where she feels secure. She's highly strung and can be spooked by the crowds. And it's only fair to show you this.' She rolled back her sleeve to show the scar—still livid where

226

the horse had bitten her.

'Magenta?' Paige ran a gentle finger over the newly healed skin. Alex nodded.

'She didn't mean to do it but it happened, anyway.'

'Horse-racing is never without any risk. That's why I wanted to see your Madge on my own without Luke huffing and puffing, telling me I couldn't do it. I thank you for your honesty, Alex, but I'm still taking the ride.'

'Good.' On impulse, Alex embraced her, feeling that she had made a new friend. 'I'll get you some coffee,' she said, not wanting to let Paige go.

'Thanks.' Paige followed her to the canteen.

When they were seated, enjoying hot coffee, Paige stopped smiling, becoming suddenly serious. 'Alex,' she said, 'can I say something personal? Even if I may be speaking out of turn? I never could mind my own business.'

'Of course,' Alex said, wondering what it could possibly be.

'Why don't you put that poor man out of his misery? Can't you see he's in love with you?'

'What? Who?'

'Grady, of course.' Paige rolled her eyes heavenwards. 'You must know how he looks at you with his soul in his eyes. But no. Sometimes it takes an outsider to see these things.'

'I'm sure you're wrong. Grady wouldn't— and we've already talked about it,' she said miserably. 'He's convinced he's too old for me.'

'By how many years?'

'I dunno. Ten. Twelve.'

'Uhuh. The same difference as there is between Luke and me.'

'But he thinks of me as a child. The one time I tried to talk to him about his past he closed up like a clam and wouldn't discuss it with me.'

'Then he still has issues with it. And you're not going to get anywhere if you don't sort it out.'

'I'm not sure that he wants me to.' Alex stirred the dregs of her coffee with her spoon. 'And there's something else you should know: I'm not a reliable person—not at all.'

'Really? You seem pretty grounded to me.'

'That's because you don't really know me. I might be in love with Grady now—you're right about that. But I'm notoriously fickle—I have to be to fall in and out of love so easily. I'm scared to trust my own feelings any more. You do know I was engaged to his brother, Jared?'

Paige shook her head, waiting for Alex to say more.

'You must've seen the tabloids? *Heir to millions dumped by stable hand! Millionaire's son ditched at the altar!*'

'No, I didn't. I never read the papers because they rely on sensationalism and rarely report the truth.' Paige stood up. 'All the same, if you do love Grady, I'll give you some advice. If he's trying to convince himself he's too old for you, the next move will have to be yours. Don't miss out on a lifetime of happiness because of false pride and foolishness. I very nearly did.'

And she stood up before Alex could gather her thoughts to question her further. 'Thanks for the coffee, Alex. I'll see you at track work tomorrow—bright and early.'

CHAPTER TWELVE

After Paige had gone, Alex brooded, spending a lot of time thinking about Grady and finding it hard to believe what her new friend had said. Of course Grady wasn't in love with her; why should he want someone who had so recently belonged to his brother? He'd think it indecent—on the verge of being incestuous. And how was she supposed to make the first move? He'd think she was crazy. Jared had rushed her into a wedding, giving her no time to think. She hadn't the first idea how to go about seducing anyone. And would she want to, even if she could? It seemed calculated somehow as well as deceitful. These things should be allowed to develop naturally. But then, leaving the whole thing to fate could result in the status quo.

229

So, on her next full day off, she drove over to Chadstone Shopping Centre to buy some new clothes. Having been so involved in her duties with Madge, she had saved most of the money she earned and hadn't indulged in a shopping spree for some time.

She was surprised to see how far fashion had moved on without her. Gone were the hipster pants and eighties-style wide belts buckled on the hip. T-shirts and crop tops weren't as prominent as before and the theme for summer appeared to be feminine with short, swirling dresses in subtle, floral shades and ankle-strapped sandals with dangerously high heels. Fifties-style cotton prints were in evidence, too.

Daunted by the dozens of racks in the department stores, she found a sympathetic assistant in a small boutique and discovered two empire-line dresses in delphinium blues and purples that flattered her dark hair. Unable to choose between them, she decided to take both. From the same shop she bought a luxurious wrap in jewel colours of two shades of purple and gold.

Having started to spend money, she found herself unable to stop and visited an underwear boutique where she started hunting through the racks. Bras and briefs had come a long way from the sensible schoolgirl white cotton she usually wore. She wrinkled her nose at the thought of her own bras, washed so many times they were turning limp and grey. She tried on beautiful, satin ones that fitted like a second skin; bras with plunging necklines in colours to match her new dresses. She was amazed by the difference they made, although the price tickets on these boutique undies made her catch her breath. Her usually trim but unremarkable figure was transformed into that of a siren and, before she could change her mind and resist temptation, the assistant drew her attention to matching briefs in several flattering designs.

Laden with packages, she checked her bank balance before going home and found she had very little money left. Feeling guilty, she was tempted to go and take everything back, but when she peeked in the bags at her purchases, she just couldn't do it. Instead she went to a department store and spent the last of her savings on a big bottle of Chanel 'Chance'. *I'm taking a chance and investing in my future* she told herself, at last beginning to believe in a future that might include Grady as well as Madge.

But when she came down to earth she found things had grown even more awkward between them. Ever since that fateful evening when she had raised the subject of his past, Grady had distanced himself; they had lost the easy, platonic relationship they had enjoyed before. He couldn't relax, even when they were alone, making small talk and asking after Vere and the baby due some time near Christmas. But usually their conversation remained on the safer topic of horses.

Having committed herself to Magenta, Paige arrived almost on a daily basis to train with the filly who was now as comfortable with her new rider as she had been with Tasha.

'Well?' Paige asked her at the end of a busy work-out and while Alex was hosing down Madge. 'How goes it with his lordship, then?'

'Quite simply, it doesn't.' Alex shrugged. 'He treats me like one of the lads. Short of pretending to faint into his arms, I don't know what else to do.'

'Leave it to me then. I'll ask you to dinner— both of you.' Paige's smile was mischievous. 'I can say I want to discuss strategy for Madge.'

'He's not likely to fall for that, is he?' Paige frowned. 'He'll say we can discuss all that here at the stables.'

'Oh, I think he will. He's probably waiting for just such an opportunity.' Paige grinned, enjoying her role as matchmaker. 'And if he won't bring you to our place for supper, then we can stop stressing about it—we'll know I got it all wrong.'

But Grady did accept Paige's dinner invitation for the following Sunday evening.

Respecting his wife's decision to ride Magenta, Luke had set aside his misgivings to become a genial host. And they weren't the only visitors at the Sandfords' table. They had house guests—Stella and Michael Kent, a middle-aged couple from England, here for the Melbourne Cup Carnival. They wanted to experience the Australian scene for themselves before deciding whether to bring a contender the following year. A typical Englishman, Michael talked in glowing terms of Australian racing, full of praise for everything he had seen so far. His wife was more reticent, contributing little to the conversation. She brightened considerably towards the end of the evening when Paige's grandmother came to the table bringing Marc, Paige's little boy.

'I just brought Marc to say goodnight—' she started to say.

'Oh no, please let him stay.' Stella got up and crouched in front of him. 'He's adorable and I didn't realize how much I should miss my own little boy.'

Marc was only five but he knew how to respond to an appreciative audience. Alex watched the easy camaraderie and love exchanged in this family group, wishing her own could be more like it. But it was too late. Mim would never be other than prickly and critical, jealous of Alex's good relationship with her father.

'All right, Alex?' Grady whispered. 'You were looking a bit solemn there for a moment.'

'I'm fine,' she smiled back at him. 'Just thinking of Mim.'

'Ooh, no.' He winced. 'You don't want to do that.'

Alex giggled.

'That's better,' he said. 'Have I told you, you're looking particularly lovely tonight. Is that a new dress?'

She nodded, enjoying the feel of the silk georgette rustling against her skin and almost blushed at the thought of the brand new sexy underclothes she was wearing beneath.

Coffee was served and, although it was only ten o'clock, it was becoming obvious that the Sandfords didn't want a late night. By half past, Grady and Alex were on their way home.

'We didn't really get to talk about Magenta—' Alex began.

'No,' Grady smiled. 'But I don't think Paige invited us there for that.'

'She wanted us to meet their overseas visitors?'

'Nope. I don't think it was that either,' he said, keeping his eyes on the road.

'What then?'

'Wait until I can find somewhere safe to stop. I don't like getting into serious conversations when I'm driving.'

'That sounds ominous.' Alex said, wondering what he could possibly want to say to her now. As a typical, old-fashioned

Australian male, he had spent most of the evening talking to Michael and Luke, leaving the womenfolk to entertain themselves. By now, Alex had convinced herself that Paige was a romantic idiot with too much time on her hands. When she saw her next, she would tease her and say she'd make a fortune writing love stories for magazines.

But instead of taking the busy main road leading back to Cranbourne, she saw Grady was leaving it to take a path so narrow that the bushes were almost scraping the sides of the big silver car.

'This used to be the path to my favourite beach,' he told her. 'It's almost overgrown now because hardly anyone uses it any more. They've made a new road that leads to a big car-park at the top of a cliff and installed a ticket machine. In the Christmas holidays, the world and his wife come here and it isn't the same.'

'Oh.' Alex didn't know what else to say. She was very conscious of his imposing presence in the seat next to her and her heart had set up an uneven beat, making it hard to speak.

Finally, the path gave way to a small patch of tarmac behind the dunes with just about room for one car to turn around. Grady pulled up as close to the shore as he could so that they could watch the waves rolling in on the deserted beach. He cut the motor and, apart from rhythmic sounds of the sea, it seemed very quiet and dark. There was just enough moonlight for them to see each other clearly. He turned towards her, placing an arm along the back of her seat—a gesture so reminiscent of Jared that she sat up straight to avoid any contact, very conscious of it lying there.

'Now then,' he said. 'I think you and Paige are up to something and I need to know what it is.'

'Nothing. What could we possibly—?'

'Don't lie. She asks us to dinner to talk about Madge and the subject never comes up. And here you are, dressed up to the nines and reeking of perfume.'

'You don't like it?'

'Of course I like it. I love it. But why? Why are you doing this to me now?'

'I'm so sorry, Grady. It was a stupid idea and I should have known that you wouldn't fall for it.'

'Are you saying you went to all this trouble just for me?'

She nodded, her eyes filling with sudden tears. 'Paige seemed to think—oh, it doesn't matter now—I feel stupid. I'm sure she was wrong.'

'What did Paige think?'

'I told you—it doesn't matter now.'

'But it does.' Gently, he placed his hand on the back of her neck. 'Or you wouldn't be so upset.'

'I'm not upset. All right, you might as well

236

know and then you can have a good laugh. Paige thinks you're in love with me—isn't that silly? And people will think I'm such an idiot. Leaving Jared only to go chasing after his brother.'

'I don't care what anyone thinks. I never did. And Paige is right. I've tried not to let it happen but I am in love with you. From the moment I set eyes on you that day in Magenta's stall.'

'You were furious with me.'

'My form of self defence. I didn't want to be in love with anyone—let alone a girl half my age.'

Alex gazed at him, trying to read his expression in the gloom. 'So why didn't you say something before? Why did you let Jared get in the way?'

'Because once you'd met him, you didn't see me at all. As if you were under a spell.'

'It's called infatuation, Grady, and has as much value as fool's gold. Everyone tried to warn me about Jared—even Katrina.'

'And I stood back because I hoped that he really did love you as I did. I didn't want to get in the way. It wasn't until much later that I found out he did it to spite me.'

'But why? Why should he do that?'

Grady shrugged. 'That's Jared for you. It's my own fault—I should've hidden my feelings better. He doesn't value anything unless someone else wants it first.'

'I see. And what do you think he'll do now?'

'I don't know. He'll have to come back to Melbourne eventually—Olivia, Morris' old PA, will make sure of that. He still has the lion's share of Pa's business and she'll see that he earns it—but I think he knows better than to show his face anywhere near the stables, or me.'

'He's still your brother, Grady. You can't shut him out of your life forever.'

'No. But I'll do my best.' Tentatively, he drew her into his arms. Everything he did was sure and deliberate. 'But I brought you here to admire my favourite beach. Not to talk about Jared.'

He kissed her then with infinite care and a lot of expertise. It wasn't their first kiss—but it was infinitely more pleasurable, everything she had always hoped it might be. She clung to him, responding to his every move.

'Lovely Alex,' he said when at last they came up for air. 'But I want you to be certain about this.'

'I couldn't be more certain.' She raised her lips to his, slightly parted, inviting him to kiss her again.

'Not now, my love.' He gave a long sigh and sat back in his seat. 'I think we should leave. Otherwise, I'm likely to tear that beautiful dress and ravish you on the spot.'

Alex realized she wasn't at all unhappy with such a thought but there was still something she needed to know; a question stored at the back of her mind. She could only hope this was the right time to raise it. Or would it ruin everything, shrivelling this newly discovered love?

'Grady, there's just one more thing. If you really do love me—'

'What can I say? I want to marry you, Alex. What more can I do to make you believe me?'

She decided to take the plunge even if he closed his mind to her as before. 'Grady I don't want any secrets between us and you already know the worst about me. I need to know why you never got married before. Why was it that you remained faithful to that long lost girl? Did you love her so much?'

He closed his eyes, shaking his head, and it was a long moment before he spoke. 'I don't like to think of it, Alex,' he said at last. 'It was a bad time and stirs up all those old feelings of shame and of guilt—'

'Guilt?' She stared at him. 'Why should you feel guilt because your fiancée died? Surely, that wasn't your fault?'

'I've always felt that it was.' He was speaking so softly, she could scarcely catch the words. 'Because although it was an accident and I never meant it to happen, I was the cause of her death.'

Alex held her breath, fearful of saying anything that might make him stop.

'And if, after you've heard the full story, you

want no more to do with me—I'll understand.'

'Grady, just tell me,' she said, taking his hand and holding on to it with both her own. 'Surely it can't be so bad.'

'Sascha came from the old country. Her father and mine were old friends and kept up a correspondence although they hadn't seen one another for many years. My father told me his friend's daughter wanted, above all things, to begin a new life in Australia. It wasn't quite a pre-arranged marriage but there was an understanding that if we liked one another, a wedding would take place.' He sighed, shaking his head. 'We went to the airport to meet her—my father and I, not knowing what to expect. Photographs can be so deceptive. I myself was still plagued with acne, even though I was past twenty, but I'd taken care to have my own photos retouched to hide the scars. But when Sascha arrived, we could scarcely believe our luck. She was even lovelier in real life—slender and pale with a face like a flower. She moved with the grace of an angel and I was enraptured right from the start. I couldn't wait to set a date for the wedding and call the banns.'

'So what happened to make everything go so wrong?'

'If she'd been shy and more reticent, I might never have guessed her true nature. But she shocked me by wanting to sleep with me almost as soon as we'd met. I didn't know how to handle it. I was naïve and rather a prig, I suppose, and she scared me. I said we needed to spend more time together before taking such a step. I told her I wanted to wait for the wedding—it was only two months away, after all.'

'When she heard this, she screamed and swore at me in several languages without repeating herself and I began to think better of marrying such a shrew. I knew it would cause a big drama and a rift between my father and his old friend but I also knew that if I went through with it, I'd regret it for the rest of my life.'

'You would, indeed. Because that girl was already pregnant with some other man's child.'

'She was. But how did you know?'

Alex shrugged. 'It figures. If she could sleep with you quickly, everyone would think the baby was yours.'

'I was nervous so I took her to a quiet place to tell her I wanted to break it off. An old picnic spot overlooking the beach. Nobody else was there. It was such a cold, windy day that the place was deserted. In hindsight, it wasn't a good choice but I was afraid she might get abusive, or even violent, and I didn't want my father—and certainly not Simone— to hear what she had to say.' His mouth twisted at the memory. 'It took some time and at least half a bottle of vodka to get her to tell me the truth. Finally, she admitted she was at least three months pregnant with her married lover's child. Far from being in love with me, she said she despised me for my pock-marked looks and for being my father's biddable, obedient son.'

'Oh, Grady.'

'Then she threatened me. She told me her father was a criminal overlord in the old country and, when he heard how his daughter had been treated, he would send someone to kill me. They were empty threats—I can see that now—but at the time I was scared—I believed them. Foolishly, then we fought. It was very clumsy and physical. She flew at me with her nails ready to tear at my eyes and I pushed her away. She came at me again and we wrestled closer and closer to the edge of the cliff where there were no barriers. I was amazed at the strength in one so slight but I suppose she was driven by rage and determination. Suddenly, it came to me that I was fighting for my life. Moving closer and closer to the edge, she was hoping to catch me in an unguarded moment and push me out over the rocks. If I died, there would be no one to say that the baby wasn't mine; my father would have to take responsibility for Sascha and her child.'

Alex closed her eyes, knowing there could be only one ending to this tale.

'It happened so quickly, I'm still not sure

242

how,' he said, clearly tormented by this final memory. 'She came running towards me with her head down, meaning to head butt me in the stomach and make me fall backwards off the cliff. If she'd caught me off balance she could have done it easily—I was only a skinny boy—but at the last second, I threw myself out of the way. Propelled by her own momentum, she flew over the edge and was gone. It happened so fast, she didn't have time to scream. When I lay flat on the ground to look over the edge, I could see her lying there broken on the rocks below. She was staring up at me with lifeless eyes, her skull cracked and the brains seeping out, the sea already lapping at the blood in her hair.' He sighed heavily once again. 'So there it is. I'm a murderer. Now you know.'

'No, no Grady.' She wanted to shake some sense into him. 'How can you possibly say this was your fault? That girl came to Australia with only one thing in mind. To set someone up as a patsy to raise her child.'

'I know. But if only I'd done things differently. If I'd tried harder to reason with her.'

'Grady, there is no reasoning with someone like that. So tell me, what happened afterwards?'

'The police grilled me because I was the only witness and there was an inquest, of course, but due to the lack of evidence, they brought in a verdict of accidental death. Then, when it came out that Sascha was pregnant, people looked askance at me for a while, believing I might have killed her because of the child. But my father left me in peace and looked for no more European brides. He lost contact with Sascha's father, of course, and I shut the door on the story and locked it away at the back of my mind. After that bad experience, I steered clear of women for many years. Until a particular black-haired girl came to my stables and fell in love with Magenta.'

'Thank you for telling me, Grady. I know what it must have cost you.'

'No. I should thank you for making me look at it. I can see things differently now. It's as if a huge burden has been lifted from my shoulders.'

Impulsively, she kissed his cheek. 'No more regrets or shadows between us now.' Enthusiastically, he took her face in his hands and kissed her back.

'Grady,' she said as if a thought had suddenly occurred to her. 'There's something I need to know. If you've steered clear of women for over ten years—'

'No,' he said quickly. 'I can see where this conversation is going. I've steered clear of emotional involvement, that's all. I'm not a thirty-year-old virgin if that's what you think.'

'So?'

'No, Alex. This time I mean it. The subject is closed.'

CHAPTER THIRTEEN

Alex had some difficulty in persuading Grady to have a secret engagement, for the time being at least. They were in Toby's office and he had just given her a beautiful single sapphire surrounded by diamonds that had belonged to his mother. It was the last token, he said—all he had left of her. Although she intended to leave him all her personal things, when Simone arrived on the scene she laid claim to everything, including his mother's jewels, and Morris was too besotted, too full of new love to prevent her. Grady remembered the time he had stolen it back, living in fear of reprisals for days but Simone never mentioned it.

'Oh Grady, it's the most beautiful thing anyone ever gave me.' She said, loving it so much more than the ostentatious diamond that she had posted back to Jared at his mother's address on the Gold Coast and with little regret. 'But don't you think—?'

'No, Alex. I don't want to hear any buts. If the old-fashioned setting doesn't appeal to you, you can always have the stones—'

'No, no, I love it just as it is. I'll need to have

245

it made bigger to fit my finger, that's all. Your mother must have had tiny hands.'

'She was tiny all over.' He smiled at the memory. 'I don't know how she managed to give birth to a hulking brute like me.'

'I'll wear it on a chain round my neck, till I can get it sized.'

'You won't keep it hidden for long. I don't want a long engagement.'

'Nor do I.' She gave him a quick kiss to reassure him. 'But I will need to tell my father about our plans before we announce it to anyone else. And I don't want a big, formal wedding. Not after what happened with—'

'No, indeed.' He interrupted her before she could mention Jared. 'And, if I have my way, we'll be married long before Christmas.'

'Maybe,' she said, as if something else were still troubling her. 'But there's Magenta to think of, as well. We haven't had much to do with the rest of the Carnival but she's racing on Emirates' Stakes Day.'

'As if I could forget.' He looked thoughtful for a moment. 'Do you really think Paige will manage her as well as Tasha?'

'Just as well, if not better. Madge trusts her.'

She hung her arm round his neck and gave him another quick kiss. 'Thank you for this beautiful ring. I love it.'

That was the moment Toby chose to return, taken aback by the sight of Alex in Grady's arms and doing his best to ignore it. 'Oops,' he said softly, turning as if to retreat.

'It's all right, Toby, you've caught us,' Grady said. 'But keep it under your hat for the time being. Alex and I are going to be married. Soon.'

'Well, I'll be. . . .' The old horseman's face creased in a smile. 'I wondered when common sense would prevail. Congratulations to you both. An' if you're happy as the missus an' me, you won't go far wrong.'

'Thanks, Toby.' Alex grinned at him and then turned to Grady. 'I really should tell my father now—and face to face, not over the phone. He's usually at home after lunch.'

'D'you want me to come with you?'

'What?' She giggled. 'Like an old-fashioned swain coming to get the father's approval? I don't think so.'

'Good,' he said and then added an afterthought. 'I do hope he'll be pleased.'

'He'd better be.' Alex said, thinking of the hard time she had given Vere when he married Mim.

*   *   *

No one seemed to be about when she arrived at her family home. Before going to the house, she visited the stables. One of Vere's lads, Pete, was sprawled on a bench outside, smoking. This told her at once that Vere wasn't home. As soon as Pete spotted Alex, he

247

threw the cigarette down and ground it out under his heel.

'Don't let my dad see you do that,' she said. 'He probably doesn't even know you smoke. You know he hates cigarettes anywhere near the stables.'

'Gonna tell on me, are ye?' Pete scowled at her.

'Not this time, no. But don't let me catch you at it again.'

Pete shrugged. 'Yer dad isn't here.'

'I gathered that. Is Mrs Hay with him or up at the house.'

'How should I know? She don't come down here.'

Alex considered leaving without visiting Mim and then realized she might have heard the jeep arrive. It would cause even more stress for her father if Mim complained that she'd driven off without looking in.

So she let herself into the house and called out 'Mim, it's me—Alex—are you home?'

At first there was no response and then Alex heard a small sound coming from up the stairs. It sounded a bit like a cry for help.

'Where are you?' she called and finally there was a faint response.

'Up here.'

Alex went up and checked out the main bedroom, but although Mim had some clothes laid out on the bed, there seemed to be nobody there.

'In here!' came the cry, louder now, and Alex realized it was coming from the en-suite.

Mim was sitting in the shower, naked and cradling her belly, her little dog sitting beside her whimpering. She had pulled the curtain down on top of herself in her efforts to get up and she was shivering and crying.

'Oh Alex, thank God you came. I was having a shower and I fell.'

'Are you all right?' Even as she said it, Alex could see it was a stupid thing to ask.

'No—or I wouldn't still be here. I fell and couldn't get up again. And now—now I think the baby's coming and it's too soon.' Shivering and hopeless, Mim started crying again. 'I can't lose our baby—not now.'

'You're not going to lose the baby. I won't let you,' Alex said, hoping she sounded a lot more confident than she felt. 'We have to get you to hospital right away.' She checked her mobile, relieved to see it was fully charged. 'I'll call an ambulance and then we'll see about getting you dry and warm.' Quickly, she made the call, stressing urgency, and then ran to the linen press for some towels. She placed some on the towel rail to heat and then set about drying Mim who was looking up at her with a doleful expression.

'I'm so sorry, Alex. This must be awful for you. I know you don't like me.'

'Liking doesn't come into it now, Mim. You're carrying Dad's baby—my little brother

249

or sister.'

'Sister, actually. According to the ultrasound.'

'Great,' Alex said, surprised to find that she meant it. She started rubbing her stepmother with the warm towels. 'I'll go and look out for the ambulance. It should be here any minute now.'

'No. Please don't leave me. I'm scared on my own.' She grasped Alex's hand in a vice-like grip.

'I'll have to go down and let them in. But while we're waiting for them, I'll call Dad.'

'He's a long way away and he's busy. Over at Werribee with the horses.'

'You and the baby are most important now. He'll want to know.'

She made a quick phone call to her father, trying to explain what had happened without alarming him. He promised to get someone else to deal with the horses and meet up with them at the hospital.

By the time the ambulance and the paramedics arrived, Mim was having severe contractions but there was still no sign of the baby's head. Alex locked the little dog in the laundry and insisted on riding in the ambulance with her.

'I'm so sorry, Alex,' Mim whispered in one of the quieter phases when she could talk. 'I was so awful to you. And you're being so kind to me now.'

250

'Mim, save your strength.' Alex whispered back, pushing the damp hair away from the older woman's face. 'We can talk about all of this when the baby's here and you're well again.'

'Yes, Alex, but if I should—'

'Hardly anyone dies in childbirth, these days, Mim. And I told you—I won't let you or your baby die.'

By the time Vere arrived at the hospital, full of anxiety and panic, his wife had been delivered of a baby girl by Caesarian section. The specialist told them the child was healthy, if a bit premature, and was now resting contentedly in a special crib in the nursery. They could see her, if they liked.

Alex looked at this tiny, red morsel of humanity whose eyes were so tightly shut they couldn't be seen, not knowing what to say. Although she knew her father expected something.

'She's beautiful, Dad,' Alex began, until he silenced her with a look. 'Well, she will be when she's older. Do you have a name for her yet?'

'No. We've been fighting over it, to be honest. Mim wants to call her Thelma.'

'That can't be lucky. Reminds me of that old film *Thelma and Louise*.'

'Exactly what I said. But apparently, Mim has a favourite aunt of that name who's promised to leave her some money.'

'Trust Mim. And just as I was beginning to warm to her, too.'

'Maybe, after your Florence Nightingale act, she'll let *you* choose a name.'

'I wouldn't count on it,' Alex smiled. Then she realized Vere was looking at the ring she was wearing on a silver chain around her neck. It had fallen out of her blouse. He picked it up to examine it more closely.

'That's very pretty—and valuable, too. But if Jared gave it to you, don't you think you should send it back?'

'It isn't from Jared, Dad, it's from Grady. That's what I came to tell you today until I got distracted, taking care of Mim. We're going to be married—'

'Oh no, you're not.'

'Why? What do you mean?' She stared at him, shocked by this immediate and negative response. 'I thought you and Grady were friends. I thought you'd be pleased.'

'Friends we may be. That doesn't mean I want him to marry my daughter. I didn't even want you to work for him.'

'No and you never said why.'

'For starters, the man's almost twice your age. And there are shadows in his past. Oh, nobody talks about them now, but at the time—'

'He told me all about the shadows, Dad, and I don't care. We really do love each other and—'

'Love! I don't think you know the meaning of the word. It's only a matter of weeks since you were besotted with his younger brother. You changed your mind quickly enough over that. How do I know you won't do so again?'

'I knew you'd say that. But I'm marrying Grady, whether you like it or not!'

'If you two don't keep your voices down, you'll have to leave.' A nurse came up to them, hands on hips and speaking in an angry whisper. 'We have very new babies here and they need their rest.'

'Sorry,' Alex mumbled, still glaring at her father.

Later, they saw Mim, who was too sleepy and euphoric to divine the frosty atmosphere between her husband and his daughter.

'How's my little Thelma?' she said, holding Vere's hand with the one that wasn't attached to a drip. 'I wish I could see her.'

'I'm sure you will. Very soon.' Alex whispered. 'But I have to go now, Mim. Tomorrow is Emirates' Stakes Day and Madge is racing for the first time in the Carnival. I have to be there for her. But I promise I'll come and see you as soon as I can.'

'Make sure you do.' Mim smiled at her. 'Thanks again, Alex. If it wasn't for you, I might be—'

'But you're not. And you and little Thelma will soon be well and back home where you belong.' She shot a narrow-eyed glance at her father and surprised him by planting a kiss on Mim's cheek.

'Alex!' he said in an urgent whisper. 'This isn't the end of it. We need to talk.'

'I don't think so, Dad. I have a very clear picture of how you feel.'

It wasn't satisfactory but there it had to be left.

* * *

When she told Grady of her father's reaction, he didn't seem all that surprised.

'I told you I should have come with you—' he started to say.

'I don't know. It might just have made things worse. You would have quarrelled with him for sure.'

'Try not to worry too much. We can't do any more about it until after Madge's big race.'

'It is a shame, though. Just as I was starting to mend fences with Mim.'

'I'm sure it isn't as bad as you think. We've shocked him, springing it on him like that. He'll get over it.'

Alex bit her lip. She wasn't so sure.

Emirates' Stakes Day dawned bright and clear. Warm weather had been forecast and when Alex arrived at Flemington, she could see that the women of Melbourne had responded by turning out in their new summer

254

finery. Only a few weeks ago, they had been wrapped up in scarves and the tired jumpers and jeans they had worn all winter. Alex, aware of the all-encompassing numbered tabard she must wear while escorting Madge, was dressed in her usual jeans, teamed today with a cool, white blouse and a sturdy, wide-brimmed bushman's hat to protect her head from the scorching sun overhead. Many visitors to the racecourse weren't as careful. White limbs were much in evidence and they would be lobster red by the end of the day unless they stayed in the shade. Others had resorted to startling spray tans, resulting in shiny, orange-coloured skin. Hats were, if anything, more feathery and ridiculous than usual, in danger of being carried off by the breeze.

She had left Grady's ring with a jeweller who had been impressed with its value and promised to do the job urgently. Having become used to wearing it on its customary chain, she missed the heavy feel of it around her neck.

Grady had visited briefly to see that Madge was settling into her temporary quarters and had not been disturbed by the noisy crowds. People who didn't know much about horses were determined to party and have a good time, not realizing that most of these animals were used to a quiet, country environment and could easily be upset by too much noise.

When he left, they gazed at each other with longing but did not kiss.

As it was Paige's only ride for the day, she had already changed into Grady's colours of purple and red with stars down the sleeves.

'Well,' she said, patting Madge who had brightened considerably at the sight of her new friend, 'how's our girl?'

'We've done the best we can with her. She's in top form and it's up to the two of you now. She's racing in a very large field.'

'It'll be OK. Grady's instructed me. I'll hang out the back and stay out of trouble, relying on Madge's phenomenal turn of speed in the straight. We're drawn mid-field and I should be able to find a space to come down the middle. They'll be watching the favourites and trying to block them or ride in beside them. Nobody will concern themselves about Madge.'

'You make it sound so easy, Paige.'

'Oh, I wouldn't want you to think that. This is the last chance for many. The last day of the Spring Carnival and everyone wants to win.'

Fortunately, the crowd had thinned a bit when it was time for Madge's race. But those that remained had been drinking all day and some were becoming rowdy and belligerent. Out of the corner of her eye, Alex could see several men being manhandled by the police and dragged away from the course as she walked Madge around the mounting yard. She

256

was grateful for the thick hedge of roses separating them from the crowd.

Grady was there, giving some last minute instructions to Paige, and finally it was time to surrender the filly to her care.

'Don't look so worried, Alex,' Paige reassured her with a smile. 'Once I get her out on the track and away from the crowds, she'll be fine.'

'How do I wish you luck? It seems awful to say 'break a leg' to a jockey—especially after what happened to Tash.'

'Then say nothing at all,' Paige said as Grady gave her a leg up into the saddle. 'You know I'll be doing my best.'

Grady escorted Alex up into the stands to watch the race. He was well aware of her tension but chose not to mention it, watching Paige ride his filly down to the starting gates.

The commencement of the race was not without drama. Everyone had to come out and the start was postponed as one of the fillies got herself trapped under the gate. It was some time before they could move her as, even when they had pulled her out, she continued to lie on the turf for several minutes, frozen in terror.

To everyone's relief, at last she got up, apparently unharmed, and the race was allowed to proceed without her.

The wide Flemington course gave equal opportunity to all the runners and, as it was only a short sprint up the straight, there would be no turns. As most of the fillies were young and untried, there was a lot of over-racing at the start. Not wanting to let the front runners get too far away from her, Paige maintained a steady pace mid-field, hoping to get Madge to produce a final burst of speed in the last hundred yards.

Her plan almost worked except one of the favourites responded to Madge's challenge and went forward as well, keeping pace with her. Paige had to use all her skills, riding high over Madge's neck and urging the filly to win almost by the force of her own will power. She kept her lead although it was close and she won by just half a head. But a win is a win, no matter the margin, and a triumphant Paige rode Magenta Magic back to scale, greeted with little applause from a crowd who had been backing the other horse. One man at the fence even turned his back.

After this win, Madge was to go for a spell until after Christmas when she would be prepared for the Autumn Carnivals. Paige promised to ride her again, any time Tasha Trussardi wasn't available.

'But I can't steal Tasha's ride,' she told them. 'It's hard enough for girl jockeys to get along as it is. But keep in touch, you two. And don't forget I want an invitation to the wedding.'

'If there is one,' Grady muttered. 'Alex's

father isn't pleased.'

'Why ever not? You two are made for each other. I've always thought so.'

Briefly, they told her the reason for Vere's misgivings.

'And I know my father,' Alex sighed. 'Once he has made his mind up, he doesn't change it.'

'Then you'll have to change it for him.' Paige said. 'Present him with a *fait accompli*. Get married quietly first and tell him afterwards. I have a friend who's a marriage celebrant—you can do it at our place.'

Grady gave her a slow smile although Alex was still looking dubious. 'Paige, you're a genius,' he said. 'We might just take you up on that.'

*   *   *

The arrangements for Alex's wedding couldn't have been more different from the first. To begin with, she had no misgivings or doubts and she wasn't to wear a massive, white ball gown or even a veil. She would be dressed in a simple but beautiful fifties' dress of heavy, cream lace that she found in town in a vintage clothing shop. The shop was small but the decorations had always fascinated her—the window filled with glamorous high heels as well as glittering diamante brooches and unusual bracelets set with jewels. On one wall

259

was a stag's head with various hats and caps irreverently draped on its antlers and on the other the flattering Annigoni portrait of the young Queen Elizabeth II. The shop assistant was pleased to hear that she needed the dress for her wedding and found her a pair of court shoes that were a perfect match. She decided she didn't want to wear a veil or even a hat.

With only two days to spare before the wedding was to take place, she told Grady she was feeling guilty about doing all this behind her father's back. They hadn't spoken since that unhappy exchange of words at the hospital. Mim and the baby had to be home by now and she hadn't yet fulfilled her promise to visit them.

As if thinking of Mim had conjured her, her mobile rang and she saw it was her stepmother calling.

'We're home now,' Mim said. 'And I'm bored to tears because unless she wants to feed, the baby sleeps all the time. When are you coming to see us?'

'How is little Thelma?' Alex asked, playing for time.

'Thelma Rose.' Mim said. 'And we're calling her mostly Rose. It's a compromise. Come and have lunch with us on Sunday. Unless you're still busy with the horse?'

Sunday! The day she was marrying Grady!

'Alex? Are you there, or have you dropped out?'

'No, no I'm still here. I'm sorry, Mim. Sunday isn't a good idea.' She was wondering if she dared take the plunge and ask them to the wedding.

'You sound odd. Now look, what's going on? Whenever I mention your name to Vere, he shuts up like a clam. Don't tell me the impossible has happened and you two have fallen out?'

'Mim, I'm sorry,' she said. 'I really can't talk about this on the phone. Is Dad at home with you now?'

'No, he's not. Gone off to Werribee again. Seems to live there, these days.'

'Then can I come and see you? Now?'

'Of course. I'm stuck here at home with a baby.' This was a glimpse of the old, prickly Mim. 'What else have I got to do? I'll give you lunch. Only a sandwich, mind.'

'A sandwich will be just fine. I'll bring you a bottle of champagne to go with it.'

Mim seemed to brighten at this. 'See you soon.'

*   *   *

Mim had prepared lunch outside on the patio. It was a warm day but there was plenty of shade. Baby Thelma Rose was lying awake in her pram nearby. Her eyes were open now—a startling cobalt blue.

'She really is beautiful,' Alex said, although

261

there was little to see but the baby's face. 'Well done, Mim.'

'I wish I could have given birth normally, though.' Her stepmother grimaced, placing the sandwiches on the table while Alex opened the champagne. 'I'm split right up the middle. I'll never be able to wear a bikini again.'

'They're not as fashionable as they were. Most people wear one piece bathing suits now. Cheers!' She gave Mim a flute, raising her own. 'Here's to you and to Thelma Rose.'

'Rose,' Mim said. 'I only put in the Thelma to please my batty old aunt.' Mim paused, fixing her with a look. 'But why are we making small talk? I want to know what's happened between you and your dad.'

'In a few words—I'm marrying Grady Allen and he doesn't want me to.'

'He's being silly. You have much more in common with Grady than his charming, wastrel younger brother.'

'Dad doesn't think so. As well as being too old for me, he says Grady has shadows in his past—'

'Who doesn't? What sort of shadows?'

Succinctly, Alex told Mim about Grady's disastrous engagement to Sascha and how badly it had ended.

'Yeah,' Mim nodded. 'I sort of remember it now. I was a cub reporter on a local rag at the time—weddings and funerals—you know.

262

There was quite a fuss about this girl—she was Russian or Czech or something. People said she might have been murdered but there wasn't enough evidence to make a case. Even so, Grady Allen took quite a while to live it down.'

'So why does Dad want to go on punishing him now? For something that happened so long ago?'

'He's being a father, that's all.' Mim shrugged.

'But all he's doing is driving a wedge between us.' Alex felt hot tears forming in her eyes 'What does he think? That Grady is some sort of Bluebeard who'll murder me, too?'

'No. He just wants to protect you.'

'And now I'm getting married on Sunday and he won't be there.'

'Sunday? You mean this coming Sunday?' Mim gave a low whistle. 'That's a bit soon. I say, you're not—?'

'Pregnant? No. Grady's old-fashioned. We haven't even made love yet.'

'Is that wise, Alex?' Mim raised an eyebrow. 'How d'you know you're compatible?'

'Oh, we're compatible all right. He has fingers to die for and he kisses like a dream.'

'Too much information!' Mim laughed. 'Oh Alex, whatever was wrong with us? Why couldn't we be friends like this before?'

'Maybe we needed Rose to be the catalyst. To be fair, I set up the barriers from day one

263

and never gave you a chance. But seriously, Mim, what am I going to do about Dad? If we get married on Sunday without telling him, he might never forgive me. But I don't want him to come to the wedding and make a scene.'

'It's a tricky situation but leave it with me. I'll do the best I can to talk him around. What time is the wedding and where?'

'Paige Sandford is lending us the bower at Warrender. She knows a marriage celebrant.'

'So the meddlesome Paige has a hand in this. I might have known.'

'And we have a special licence—the wedding's to take place at noon.'

'I can't promise you anything, Alex, but I'll do my best to have him there—and in the right frame of mind.'

The baby was needing attention and starting to cry. Alex stood up and hugged her stepmother, taking this as her signal to leave.

CHAPTER FOURTEEN

Alex awoke to a wedding day bright and clear—the air so still it held the promise of being hot. She had come to Warrender the previous night to stay with Paige and her family before taking her vows the following day. This was the first time she had spent any time with Paige's grandmother, Nanou, who proved to be quick-witted as anyone half her age and with a world of wisdom about race-horses. The only note of sadness was that she'd had no word from Mim in the days since she'd seen her. She checked her mobile phone yet again to make sure she hadn't missed any messages. Still there was nothing.

The phone rang while it was in her hand and her heart thumped, expecting it to be Mim. It wasn't. It was her cousin, Jen.

'You're a dark horse, Alex!' She burbled. 'Leaving it till the last minute to tell me. But I've still got that bridesmaid's dress if you want to press me into service again.'

'Oh, Jen, I'm sure that wouldn't be lucky—not after what happened last time. This is going to be a very small affair—no best man and no bridesmaids.'

'Well, if there's not going to be a best man, there's no point in being your bridesmaid, is there?' Jen was still convinced that if she were the bride's attendant, she should be allowed first crack at the best man.

'Just come as an ordinary guest, Jen. I'm sure you'll have a good time.'

*　　*　　*

An hour or so later, she had given up all hope of hearing from Mim or Vere. She would just have to get married without her father's blessing, allowing time to mend their differences. Surely he would relent when he saw how happy she was?

Paige became brisk and businesslike when she saw the bride looking thoughtful at the breakfast table, almost on the verge of tears.

'Come on now, Alex,' she said. 'Not having second thoughts are you? Not thinking of becoming a serial runaway bride?'

'Of course not.' Alex smiled and brushed away the tears with her fingers. 'It's just that I thought Mim could talk my father around. I should have heard from them by now.'

'Don't worry. Luke is quite willing to stand in at the last minute and give you away.'

'Thank you, Paige. You've all been incredibly kind. Your grandmother, too.'

'Oh, Nanou is an old romantic at heart. Nothing pleases her more than an impromptu wedding.'

And at last it was time. Although Jen wasn't a bridesmaid, she had insisted on doing the bride's hair and make-up and Alex knew she was looking her best as she walked down the stairs and towards the front door where Luke was waiting to escort her.

'I hope Grady knows how lucky he is,' he said, tucking her arm into his. 'You make a beautiful bride.'

'She does but there's still something missing.' This was an agonized cry from Paige. 'Did no one think to get you some flowers? We can't have a bride without flowers. Wait and I'll pick some of Nanou's roses.' And she grabbed the secateurs kept in the old hall seat and ran out into the rose garden to make a quick raid on the garden. Pierre de Ronsard yielded plenty of fat pink and white blooms and she returned in minutes, snatching a ribbon from Jen's hair to bind them.

'Sorry,' she said when Jen squealed, clutching at her now unruly curls. 'But this is an emergency.'

Ready at last and trying to ignore the odd earwig among her flowers, Alex allowed Luke to lead her towards the small group that awaited them in the shade of the rose bower at the far end of the garden.

The marriage celebrant, a handsome, older man with iron grey hair, was waiting to greet them. Grady was already standing there, ramrod straight and rather tense, she thought. No doubt he was recalling that other disastrous wedding day only a few months before.

'Gather round, people.' The wedding celebrant raised his arms, inviting everyone to move closer. 'Don't hang back and be shy. This is a small intimate occasion for the closest friends of Alex and Grady but no less significant than a Royal wedding in front of thousands of witnesses.' He paused then, frowning and looking in the direction of the house. Everyone had heard a car drawing up in the midst of a wave of gravel and a squeal of brakes.

Alex turned to see her father jump out of the car and come running across the lawn towards them. Mim climbed out more slowly and followed at a more leisurely pace, carrying the baby in her arms.

'Stop the wedding!' Vere called out 'Wait for me, please.'

'Oh, Dad,' Alex groaned, casting a despairing glance at Grady. 'I couldn't get married without telling him—but this is what I was afraid of.'

'Alex, am I in time? You're not married yet, are you?'

Miserably, she shook her head.

'I hope you'll forgive me—both of you'—he glanced at Grady, including him in the apology—'because if you'll allow me, Alex, I've come to give you away.'

Smiling, Luke stood back, allowing Alex's father to take his place by her side. From that moment all the shadows rolled away and Alex felt truly able to celebrate what was now the happiest day of her life.

The ceremony was brief but sincere and afterwards, Jen caught the makeshift bouquet, retrieved her ribbon and gave the roses to Paige to put in a vase. Caterers had been engaged to serve a buffet lunch in the large, formal dining room at the house.

'Mim, you're a miracle worker,' she said to her stepmother as soon as they were free to speak alone. Vere was engrossed, talking horses to Luke Sandford who was thinking of obtaining some polo ponies of his own.

'I second that with all my heart,' Grady said with his arm around Alex. He didn't seem to want to let his bride out of his sight. 'But how did you do it?'

'Oh, I told him I wouldn't stand for it.' Mim smiled, shrugging one shoulder. 'And I gave him a hard time. I said I hadn't gone to the trouble of making friends with his daughter just to have him alienate her again. I called him a stubborn, stiff-necked old fool and that if he wouldn't come to the wedding and do his duty as a father, I might even leave him.'

Alex gasped. 'But you didn't mean it?'

'Of course not. But he's too much in love with Thelma Rose to go calling my bluff.'

'What happened to her?' Grady whispered to Alex, when Mim had left them and was showing the baby to Nanou. 'She's gone from waspish to wonderful overnight.'

'Motherhood,' Alex said. 'Thank heaven for Thelma Rose.'

'Ah,' he said, looking thoughtful. 'So if you ever start getting shrewish towards me, all I have to do is—'

'Don't even think about it,' she said. 'I do want children eventually, yes. But not any time soon.'

*   *   *

269

There had been little time for Grady to arrange a honeymoon in an exotic location, but somehow he achieved it. He would tell Alex no more than they were bound for an exclusive resort somewhere in the Whitsunday Islands off the North Queensland coast. It was an eco retreat and she would need only light, casual clothing as well as some swimsuits.

Alex wasn't nervous of flying although she had done little, apart from going on a school expedition to Sydney several years ago when the *Lord of the Rings* costumes and props were on show at a museum. She never felt sick in the air but felt ill immediately if she had to travel on water.

'We're not going by boat, are we?' she asked tentatively.

'Nothing so mundane. We'll be collected by helicopter from the mainland and taken to the resort. I believe they drop us directly on to the beach.'

'Oh, Grady,' she sighed, leaning against him 'I can hardly believe that it's happened and we really are married.' She gazed at her new wedding ring, made of similar gold to the ring that had belonged to Grady's mother.

For going away, she had chosen one of the light but glamorous dresses she had bought on that extravagant shopping expedition—the one that Grady hadn't so far seen.

Ready to leave, she embraced Paige, Luke

and Nanou, thanking Paige especially for making everything possible. Marc insisted on giving her a sticky kiss mixed with a mouthful of wedding cake.

Her father hugged her and shook hands with Grady. 'Don't know what got into me,' he said, still somewhat embarrassed. 'Took my wife to make me see sense.'

Alex hugged Mim and dropped a kiss on the head of the sleeping Thelma Rose.

'I must thank you again,' she whispered. 'None of this would have happened except for you.'

'Oh, nonsense, Alex.' Mim was brisk. 'Vere would have come round eventually.'

'Maybe,' Alex said. 'But not in time to give me away. Now we have that memory and it's on film, too, so no one can take it away.'

As they were due to fly out at 10 a.m. the following morning, Grady had booked a luxurious bedroom at one of the best hotels in town.

'Now,' he said to his new wife, as they piled their cases into the Mercedes and set off for town. Fortunately, as it was a small, quiet wedding, no one had thought to decorate the car. 'Our honeymoon starts here and I don't want to hear one more word about Madge for the whole duration.'

'But Grady, Mike doesn't always—I really should check in every day or so to make sure that she's happy.'

'And what are you going to do if she's not? Cut short the honeymoon? No, Alex. I've already asked Tasha to go down to Cranbourne each day to keep an eye on her and make sure Mike is spoiling her as she deserves.'

'But Tasha's on crutches still—she won't be able to—'

'Stop. Now. Or we're going to have the first argument of our married life.'

Alex threw up her hands and shook her head, smiling helplessly.

An hour or so later when they arrived at the hotel, porters rushed to claim their luggage and valet park the Mercedes. Alex felt slightly daunted by all this efficiency. Jared had dazzled her with luxury before and now Grady seemed to be doing the same thing. She was quiet as they took a dizzying ride in the lift to one of the higher floors. Soft carpet everywhere deadened all sound.

'All right,' Grady said softly, when they were at last alone. Alex was gazing at the fruit basket and chilled bottle of vintage champagne standing beside it. 'What's up? I always know when you're not happy.'

'Not happy? Oh Grady, how could I not be happy, married to you? I'm just used to a much simpler lifestyle.'

'So I needn't have gone to all this trouble or book an eco retreat? You'd have been just as happy with a tent on the beach, mosquitoes and all?'

'No, I didn't mean that. It's just that this is a bit overwhelming.'

'You're tense as anything.' Gently, he massaged the taut muscles at the base of her neck. 'Go and take a warm bath while I have a shower.'

Gratefully, she did so, immersing herself in the lavender-scented water. Lavender always did have a calming influence. She was completely relaxed and almost on the borders of sleep when Grady came to collect her. He was wearing one of the hotel's white bathrobes and smelled delicious.

'Come on, sleepyhead,' he said softly. 'Let's get you out before you drown in there.'

She allowed him to lift her out and envelop her in warm towels before carrying her to the enormous bed where he proceeded to dry her limbs as if she were a child.

As if at a given signal, he stopped and, suddenly serious, they gazed into each other's eyes.

'I love you, Alex,' he whispered, kissing her so softly that it felt like nothing more than the sweep of a butterfly's wings. 'You make me so happy. I feel so utterly blessed that you have come into my life.'

She could wait for no more gentleness but sprang into his lap, straddling him and kissing him deeply, her small, athletic breasts pressed hard against his chest. 'I love you, too,' she said. 'More than I ever thought possible.'

They made love, then, taking it slow and leisurely, delighting in the pleasure they gave and received from one another. Grady was a considerate lover and was quick to learn what most pleased her. This went on for most of the night until they fell asleep in each other's arms in the early hours of the morning.

They didn't stir until they were woken by the insistent ringing of the telephone.

'Yeah?' Grady answered it.

'Eight o'clock call, sir and madam,' said a horribly cheerful voice from the front desk. 'You'll need to leave soon if you're catching a ten o'clock flight.'

Laughing helplessly at the way they had overslept, they showered together, resisting the urgent temptation to make love again. They grabbed some coffee but there was no time for proper breakfast; they needed to get on their way.

Exhausted, they slept on the flight to Brisbane before joining another flight that would take them to Proserpine, the gateway to the Whitsunday Coast. From there they joined the helicopter that would drop them right there on the beach at Paradise Bay.

Looking down at the Whitsunday Islands, Alex was entranced. These islands were indeed a paradise, set in a turquoise tropical sea so clear that she could see the coral reefs just below the surface.

274

'What is it?' She sensed that Grady was watching her own expression rather than gaze at the spectacular scenery below.

'Don't ever lose that sense of wonder, Alex,' he said, taking her hand and kissing it. 'I wish we could halt time and stay in this moment forever.'

'But there will be so many other moments, Grady.' She wanted to jolt him out of this contemplative, half melancholy mood. 'And we'll have the rest of our lives to enjoy them.'